"Come out with me tonight," he whispered against her cheek. "You cannot refuse me."

"I won't turn on him," she gasped, still trembling with the shock of desire. "Not for any price. You won't kiss a betrayal out of me."

"Stubborn and foolish," he repeated softly, rubbing his thumb lightly against her swollen lower lip. "Why do you resist me?"

Her heart pounded.

"Fair warning, Grace," he said quietly. "I will seduce you tonight."

Caught in his gaze, she couldn't breathe. Her heart felt about ready to explode from her chest.

"You're welcome to try," she managed, over the rapid pounding of her heart. "I will resist you."

He gave her a slow, seductive smile. "I would expect nothing less."

Jennie Lucas grew up dreaming about faraway lands. At fifteen, hungry for experience beyond the borders of her small Idaho city, she went to a Connecticut boarding school on scholarship. She took her first solo trip to Europe at sixteen, then put off college and travelled around the US, supporting herself with jobs as diverse as gas station cashier and newspaper advertising assistant. At twenty-two she met the man who would be her husband. After their marriage she graduated from Kent State with a degree in English. Seven years after she started writing she got the magical call from London that turned her into a published author.

Since then life has been hectic, with a new writing career and a sexy husband and two small children, but she's having a wonderful (albeit sleepless) time. She loves immersing herself in dramatic, glamorous, passionate stories. Maybe she can't physically travel to Morocco or Spain right now, but for a few hours a day, while her children are sleeping, she can be there in her books. Jennie loves to hear from her readers. You can visit her website at www.jennielucas.com, or drop her a note at jennie@jennielucas.com

THE CHRISTMAS LOVE-CHILD

BY
JENNIE LUCAS

First published in Great Britain 2009
Harlequin Mills & Boon Limited,
Eton House, 18-24 Paradise Road, Richmond, Surrey TW9 1SR

© Jennie Lucas 2009

ISBN: 978 0 263 20824 5

Set in Times Roman 10½ on 12¼ pt
07-0809-42600

Harlequin Mills & Boon policy is to use papers that are natural,
renewable and recyclable products and made from wood grown in
sustainable forests. The logging and manufacturing process conform
to the legal environmental regulations of the country of origin.

Printed and bound in Great Britain
by CPI Antony Rowe, Chippenham, Wiltshire

THE CHRISTMAS
LOVE-CHILD

To my wonderful parents, who taught me to love books
and dream of faraway lands.

CHAPTER ONE

JUST when Grace Cannon thought her day couldn't get any worse, she came up from the Tube carrying £1,000 worth of lingerie for her boss's fiancée and got splashed in the face by a passing Rolls-Royce.

Mid-December in London was frosty in the violet twilight. The rain had turned to sleet, but the sidewalks in Knightsbridge were still packed with shoppers. The icy spray of gutter water hit Grace's body like a slap. She stumbled and fell down, her hip hitting the pavement as the shopping bag tumbled into the street. She cried out, holding up her hands to protect her face from the endless crush of feet pushing forward.

"Get back. Get back, damn you."

A tall, dark stranger pushed apart the crowds with his broad arms, giving Grace space to breathe. He towered over her on the sidewalk, black-haired and broad-shoul-dered in an expensive black cashmere coat.

He turned to face her.

Electric gray eyes stood out sharply against his olive-hued skin. Every inch of him whispered money and power, from his Italian shoes to the muscular shape beneath his black coat and gray pin-striped suit. His lush masculine beauty was like none she'd ever seen before. He had chiseled cheekbones, a strong jawline and a Roman profile. Her gaze fell unwillingly to his mouth, to the sensual lips that curved as he looked down at her.

A bright halo of sunlit clouds silhouetted his black hair as he extended his hand.

"Come."

Dazzled, Grace reached up and placed her hand in his far-larger one. As the handsome stranger pulled her to her feet, she felt a current run through her body more startling than the icy water that had splashed her.

"Thank you," she whispered.

Then she recognized him and literally lost her breath.

Prince Maksim Rostov.

Her throat closed.

She looked again. There could be no mistake.

Prince Maksim Rostov was the man who had saved her.

The lavishly wealthy prince was the most famous Russian billionaire in a city that was full of them. He was so ruthless in his business and personal life he made Grace's boss look like a saint in comparison. For the past two months, since the prince had broken up with his famous fiancée, he'd been photographed with a new woman every night.

Prince Maksim Rostov. Her boss's main rival. His worst enemy.

And that had been *before* last month, when Alan had stolen both the man's fiancée and his merger!

"Forgive me." The prince's cool gray eyes looked

down at her gravely, searing through her like a laser. "It was my car that splashed you. My driver should have been more careful."

"That's…all right," Grace managed to say, utterly conscious of his larger hand still closed over her own. A few minutes before, she'd been icy cold. But her body was rapidly thawing.

Warming.

Boiling.

She tried to pull away. She shouldn't let him touch her. She shouldn't even let him *talk* to her. She was two blocks away from the Knightsbridge town house she shared with her boss. If Alan ever found out that his most trusted secretary had been speaking in private with Prince Maksim, he'd never forgive her. And Grace desperately needed Alan in a good mood, tonight of all nights!

But even knowing this, she found herself unable to pull her hand from the prince's grasp. He was like a rugged, brutal, smooth old-style movie star. Like Rudolph Valentino from the 1920s, seducing women ruthlessly in a savage world of blood and sand. Like a dark angel, sent to lure innocent, helpless virgins to their destruction!

His grip tightened over hers, sending little sizzling currents up her arm, warming her beneath her wet coat.

"I will take you home."

Her teeth chattered. "I…" She shook her head. "No. It's really not necessary."

Prince Maksim pulled her close. He stroked the length of her arm, languorously brushing excess water from her coat sleeve. Feeling his hand move over her clothed body, she suddenly felt so hot she might as well have been lying naked on a California beach. Her skin burned where he touched, as if whipped by a fierce Santa Ana wind.

"I insist."

Beads of sweat formed between her breasts. "No, really," she managed. "I live close. It won't take me long to walk."

He looked down at her, a smile tracing his cruel, sensual mouth. "But I want to take you."

And still he held her hand. Her mouth went dry. Even Alan, the boss she'd loved with hopeless yearning for two years, had never sparked a response like this— never caused her nerve endings to jumble with such an intensity of feeling. Even before he'd taken a new fiancée and asked Grace to buy his Christmas gift…

The lingerie!

Grace gasped, twisting her head to the right and left.

With a little cry, she saw the Leighton bag get nailed by a swerving black cab in the road, causing the embossed lavender box inside it to tumble into the bumper-to-bumper traffic. "Oh, no!"

Ripping away from the prince's grasp, Grace pushed through the tourists to the edge of the sidewalk, looking both ways on the street and preparing to duck between the cars, double-decker buses and black cabs.

But Prince Maksim blocked her with one strong arm in front of her chest.

"Are you suicidal?" His English was perfect, with an accent she couldn't quite place. A little bit British, a bit American, with a slight inflection of something more exotic. He glanced out at the busy road. "You'd risk your life for that blue box?"

"That box," she snapped, "is my boss's Christmas gift for his new fiancée. Silk Leighton lingerie. I can't go back without it!"

"Your boss isn't worth dying for."

"My boss is Alan Barrington!"

Glaring at him, Grace waited for a reaction when he realized she worked for his enemy, his rival in the gas and oil industry, who'd not only just stolen his merger with Exemplary Oil PLC but had stolen his fiancée, the beautiful, tempestuous Lady Francesca in the bargain!

Prince Maksim's handsome face was utterly impassive. She had no idea what he was thinking. A marked difference from Alan, Grace thought. Her flirtatious boss's thoughts were always instantly expressed, either by flippant words or the expression on his good-looking face.

But the image of her boss's toothy smile dissipated instantly from her mind as the dark Russian prince reached out his hand to lift her chin, forcing her eyes to meet his. "Your boss is truly not worthy of your sacrifice."

She licked her lips nervously. "Aren't you w-wishing you'd let me run into traffic now, Your Highness?"

Prince Maksim arrogantly smiled down at her.

"As tempting as it is to cause him staffing problems, I'm afraid I cannot allow you to cover the street with your blood." He gently stroked her hair from her face. "Call me old-fashioned."

He knew she worked for his enemy, so why was he still being courteous? Why wasn't he calling her names or wishing her to the devil? Although, he would have an easy time luring any woman anywhere, she thought. Even to the depths of hell itself.

Frightened by all the new sensations running through her at his touch, she pulled back. "I'll take my chances with the traffic."

"You'll get new lingerie."

"New lingerie?" Safely out of his reach, she regained her equilibrium enough to give an incredulous, scornful laugh. "Right! New lingerie. Maybe in your world Leighton clothes are disposable as baby wipes, but—"

"I will pay for it." He gave her a level look from his steel-gray eyes. "Of course."

If it had been any other person on the planet, she would have accepted gratefully. But not this man. She couldn't accept the help of her boss's worst enemy.

Could she?

As if in slow motion, she saw a red double-decker bus crush the lavender-blue box into a big greasy puddle in the middle of the street.

Alan would be furious if she went home tonight with the expensive charge on his credit card but no lingerie. Alan was completely unforgiving of others' mistakes when they caused him problems. For years he'd hated Prince Maksim, the rival who'd beaten him over and over again. With Cali-West Energy Corporation's stock prices falling, the stockholders had begun to call for Alan's replacement as CEO.

That was before Alan met Lady Francesca Danvers at a charity ball six weeks ago. Their whirlwind romance had gained him the support of her father, the Earl of Hainesworth, who was chair of Exemplary's board of trustees. The deal had changed from a merger of British and Russian energy giants to a British-American one. For weeks now Alan had gleefully re-counted to Grace how he'd finally beaten his rival.

Grace hadn't particularly enjoyed his gloating, since it inevitably involved details of how Alan was luring the beautiful, feisty, redheaded Lady Francesca into his bed.

What if Alan was so furious about the ruined lingerie, he demanded Grace pay the bill? What if instead of giving her the advance she so desperately needed, he docked her pay?

She swore under her breath.

"Do not refuse my help, Miss Cannon," Prince Maksim said evenly. "That would be stubborn and foolish."

"Well, Stubborn and Foolish are my middle names!" Grace snapped, furious at herself.

She could have stayed in L.A. and made sure her mother's mortgage was paid each month—but no. She'd been too stubbornly and foolishly infatuated with her boss. *Pathetic,* she thought in disgust. There surely had to be some kind of self-help program for women like her, pathetically in love with a boss who believed her to have no feelings—like an animatronic robot!

"Stubborn and Foolish, Miss Cannon?" Maksim's lips curved. "Clearly American baby-name trends have changed over the years."

"My middle name is actually Diana." Narrowing her eyes, she looked up at Prince Maksim. "But you already know that, don't you? How do you already know my last name?"

"You told me you work for Barrington." He lifted a

dark eyebrow. "Don't you think I know the name of his most trusted secretary?"

Prince Maksim Rostov knew her name.

The fact made her feel warm all over. Made her feel…important.

Until a new, chilling suspicion went down her spine.

He knew her name.

He knew she worked for Alan.

And she was supposed to believe they'd just randomly met on the street two blocks from her home?

Grace was distracted and was nearly knocked over by two heavy tourists decked in cameras, Harrods bags and Santa hats, but she steadied herself to glare at him. "So you'll understand why, as his most trusted secretary, I can't accept any favors from you."

Prince Maksim gave her an easy smile.

"Barrington has nothing to do with this. Replacing the lingerie is repaying a personal debt to you." His smile spread into a carelessly wicked grin that she felt down to her toes. "I can hardly remain indebted to my enemy."

She swallowed, hardly able to collect her thoughts beneath the intensity of his gaze. "I wouldn't say I'm exactly your enemy…"

"Then there is no problem."

"But…"

He enfolded her hand back in his own. The warmth of his naked palm against hers was more erotic than she'd ever thought holding a hand could be. After so many years of useless pining over her boss, this was the most physically intimate she'd been with any man since…since…

Since that brief moment after the Halloween party

when Alan had drunkenly taken her in his arms and given her a big wet kiss before he'd collapsed in a drunken stupor on the office couch.

That sad event had been her first—and only—kiss. In school she'd been too focused on her studies to date anyone. After her father had died and she'd dropped out of college, she'd been too grief-stricken. Then she'd been too busy as a temp in downtown L.A., working to take care of her heartbroken mother and younger brothers.

Grace had become a twenty-five-year-old virgin.

A freak of nature.

And a million miles away from Prince Maksim Rostov's league!

But his car had splashed her, she argued with herself. He'd caused her to drop the lingerie. Wouldn't it be fair to allow him to replace it, when the alternative could mean her ruin?

Tempted, she licked her lips nervously. The sensation of his hand against her own caused a swirling in the tender center of her palm that sent awareness prickling up to the flesh of her ear, tightening her nipples and making her breasts feel strangely heavy. She felt his gaze trace her lips. Her cheeks went hot and her mouth went dry. Every breath she took, every rise and fall of her lungs, became more shallow.

"It is cold," he said. "My car is waiting."

"But, but Leighton clothes are expensive," she stammered, floundering. "They're so expensive they make Hermès and Louis Vuitton look like a bargain-basement fire sale."

He lifted his dark eyebrows.

"I think I can handle the expense," he said dryly. Signaling with one hand, he put the other against the small of her back, guiding her gently toward the curb of a side street where she saw a black Rolls-Royce limousine.

She felt his hand on her back and shook all over. It was that touch which finally forced her surrender.

Looking back at him, she whispered, "Alan must never know."

His lips trembled on the brink of a smile. "Agreed."

The shock waves from his hand on her lower back continued to sizzle up her arms and down her legs as she breathed, "Thank you."

"Thank you." His eyes gleamed down at her. "I always enjoy the company of a beautiful woman."

It broke the spell. She started to laugh, snorting through her nose before she covered it with a cough.

Her…beautiful? That was a good joke! She knew she wasn't anything special. And at the moment, wearing no makeup, with a damp old coat over her second-hand skirt suit and her hair tucked back in a soaked blond ponytail, she looked like a half-drowned refugee from an office in a swamp!

So why had a handsome prince dropped out of the sky to help her? Just because his driver had splashed her with water from the street? Did he have that much honor and generosity of Christmas spirit?

Or was it something else?

The dark suspicion returned to her. When she was younger, she'd believed the best of people. But since she'd started working for Alan, she'd seen how devious people could be. Both in business and in love.

Was Prince Maksim hoping to use her against Alan to take back his merger and his marriage?

"I hope you know," she said evenly, "that doing me this favor won't make me discuss Alan or the merger."

He just gave her a darkly assessing smile. "Do you think I need your assistance?"

"Don't you?" she said uncertainly.

They reached the Rolls-Royce limousine purring next to the curb. With a dismissive shake of his head to the driver, the prince opened her door himself.

"Get in."

Standing on the edge of the sidewalk, against the ebb and flow of Christmas shoppers, Grace looked at the open door of the car and hesitated. She wondered suddenly if she was doing a foolish thing, making a deal with the devil.

When she didn't move, he said mockingly, "Surely you're not afraid of me, Miss Cannon?"

Biting her lower lip, she glanced up at his handsome face. She *was* afraid of him. Afraid of his wealth, his power and well-known ruthlessness.

But even more than that, she was afraid of the sensual reaction that overwhelmed her body every time he touched her. Every time he even *looked* at her.

She shook her head uneasily. "No," she lied. "I'm not afraid of you at all."

He held the door wider. "Then get in."

Flurries of sleet swirled around Grace in a sudden gust of wind. Wet tendrils of blond hair whipped against her cheek, sticking to her skin. But she didn't feel the chill. His gray eyes seared through hers, sapping her will.

And she made her choice—which was really no choice at all. She climbed into the back seat of his Rolls-Royce.

He closed the door behind her.

Once released from his basilisk gaze, alone in the back seat, Grace was as suddenly shocked as if she'd just woken up sleepwalking in Buckingham Palace. What was she doing here? It wasn't a dream. She was really in Prince Maksim's limo. She was consorting with the enemy.

But he's not my *enemy,* she thought in confusion as she watched his dark shadow walk around to the other side. *He's Alan's enemy. And what do people say? The enemy of my friend is my enemy? Or is it that the enemy of my enemy is my friend?*

The door opened, and the most handsome, ruthless man in London climbed in beside her with a dark glance that made her feel hot and sweaty all over.

"Why are you being so nice to me?" she asked.

"Am I being nice?"

"If it's to get secrets about my boss—"

"It's Christmas. The season of joy." Festive lights from the nearby shops glinted off his wolflike teeth as he gave her a sharp smile. "And I'm going to give you joy." He turned to his chauffeur. *"Davai."*

The shadowy Rolls-Royce swept away from the curb. And just like that, Prince Maksim Rostov took her away from the drudgery and crowds and cold, and swept Grace up into his lavish world.

CHAPTER TWO

MAKSIM glanced down at the girl's lovely, dazzled blue eyes as his chauffeur drove east through the crowded traffic on Knightsbridge Road towards Mayfair. She'd called him "nice." He repeated the word in his mind as if he were trying to comprehend it.

Nice?

Prince Maksim Ivanovich Rostov had not become powerful by being nice.

His great-grandfather had been nice during his Paris exile, spending money as if he were still Grand Duke with his own fiefdom in St. Petersburg, giving largesse freely to every hard-luck story that walked into his pied-à-terre.

His grandfather had been nice, spending what little remained of the Rostov fortune down to the last penny in London as he waited impatiently for the Russian people to kick out the Soviets and beg him to return.

His father had been nice, hopelessly trying to support his young, sweet American wife by taking increasingly humiliating jobs until he'd finally followed his father's lead of suicide-by-vodka, leaving his gentle wife, eleven-year-old son and baby daughter to fend for themselves in her native Philadelphia.

But Maksim…

He was not nice.

He was selfish. He was ruthless. He took what he wanted. It was how he'd built a billion-dollar fortune out of nothing.

And now…he wanted Grace Cannon.

For the past hour, he'd been waiting for her. His chauffeur had driven back and forth on Brompton Road, waiting to catch the girl as she came up from the Knightsbridge Tube stop on the way home to her basement flat in Barrington's town house.

This young American secretary was the key to everything.

She would help him finally crush Barrington. The man had been a thorn in his side for far too long, and now he'd finally crossed the line by taking both the deal—and the woman—that rightfully belonged to Maksim.

Barrington thought he'd saved himself from ruin by taking Francesca as his fiancée. He'd soon find it was his last mistake. He would get neither the bride nor the merger.

Maksim would destroy him. As he deserved.

And Grace Cannon would help him. Whether she wanted to or not.

Maksim turned to her with a smile. Unfolding a soft cashmere blanket, he draped it over her shivering body.

"Thank you," she said, her teeth still chattering.

"It's my pleasure."

"You're not what I expected," she whispered,

pressing the blanket against her cheek. "You're not like everyone says."

"What do they say?" He carelessly placed his arm on the leather seat behind her. She was still shivering. He moved closer. Even though she was now covered with a blanket, her shivering only increased when he touched her.

"They say…you're a…ruthless playboy," she said haltingly. "That you spend half your time conquering business rivals…and the other half making conquests of women."

He laughed. "They are right." He moved closer, looking down into her face. "That is exactly who I am."

His thigh brushed against hers, and she nearly jumped out of her skin. She scooted away from him as if he'd burned her.

She was skittish. Very skittish.

There were only three possible explanations.

One—she was afraid of him. He dismissed that idea out of hand. She wouldn't have agreed to get in his car if she'd been truly afraid.

Two—she had no experience with men. He dismissed that idea, as well. A twenty-five-year-old virgin? Almost impossible in this day and age. Particularly since she not only worked for Alan Barrington, she lived in his house. He surely had seduced her many times over.

That left only the third possibility. She was ripe for Maksim's conquest.

He slowly looked her over. She wasn't a girl that any man would immediately notice. Compared to fiery bird-of-paradise Francesca, who had bright-red hair, sharp red nails and a vicious red mouth, Grace Cannon was a drab sparrow, pale and frumpy with barely a word to say for herself.

And yet…

Now that Maksim really looked at her, he saw that the girl wasn't nearly as plain as he'd first thought. Her ill-fitting coat and wet ponytail had made her seem so, but now he realized his mistake.

The fact that she wore no makeup only revealed the perfection of her creamy skin. Her eyelashes and eyebrows were so light as to be invisible, but that proved the glorious pale gold of her hair came from nature, not a salon. She wore no lipstick and her teeth hadn't been bleached to blinding movie-star whiteness, and yet her tremulous smile was warmer and lovelier than any he'd seen. She wasn't stick thin as the strange fashion for women dictated, but her ample curves only made her more lushly desirable.

He suddenly realized the dowdy secretary was a beauty.

A *secret* beauty, disguising herself away from the world. Beneath the unattractive clothing and the frumpy, frizzy hairstyle, her loveliness shone bright as the sun.

She hid her beauty. Why?

"What's wrong?" She frowned up at him suddenly, furrowing her brow in alarm.

Had she guessed his plan? "What, *solnishka mayo?*"

"You're staring at me."

"You're beautiful," he said simply. "Like sunshine in winter."

She blushed, biting her tender pink lip as she looked away. Clutching the luxurious cashmere like a security blanket against her wet, threadbare coat, she scooted further away from him on the car's leather seat. With a swallowed sigh, she stared out through the window at the passing Christmas lights beneath the thickly falling sleet. "Don't be ridiculous. I know I'm not pretty."

She didn't know, he realized. She had no idea. She wasn't purposefully hiding her beauty. *She didn't know.*

"You are beautiful, Grace," he said quietly.

At the use of her first name, she gave him a sudden fierce, sharp glance. "Don't waste your flattery on me, Your Highness."

He gave her an easy smile. "Call me Maksim. What makes you think it's flattery?"

"You might be London's most famous playboy, but I'm not that gullible. A few false compliments won't make me blurt out details about the merger with Exemplary Oil. Alan has Lord Hainesworth's support now. You won't be able to win."

So she was intuitive, as well as lovely. He was growing more intrigued by the moment. "I wasn't lying."

"I'm not a total fool. I know I'm not beautiful. There's only one reason you'd say I am."

"And that is?"

"You want me to betray Alan." She lifted her chin. "I won't. I'd die first."

"Loyalty," he said, staring at her with even greater interest. The girl felt something for her boss beyond what he'd expected. Was it possible she was in love with Alan Barrington?

A pity if the little secretary believed herself in love with him, Maksim thought. He'd just been starting to respect her.

Would money be enough to convince Grace to turn on her lover? Or would Maksim have to seduce her away from him?

Seducing a woman who was in love with another man would be an interesting challenge, he thought. And poetic justice.

But Maksim's interest in Grace was no longer just about revenge. It was no longer just about rivalry or honor.

He suddenly wanted to peel away the deceptive layers of the little secretary's plain clothing. To see her true beauty. To see her naked in his bed. To feel her lush curves against his body and see her bright, unadorned face breathless in the soft pink light of dawn.

Beneath his gaze, her pale cheeks went slowly red, like the blood-colored sun burning through the thick morning mist on the wide snowy fields of his Dartmoor estate. He watched as she nervously licked her full, pink, heart-shaped lips. Her white, even teeth nibbled at her lower lip, followed by a small dart of her tongue to moisten each corner of her mouth.

He felt himself go hard watching her.

He prayed she'd refuse his honest offer of money. Then he could just take her. Without conscience. Without remorse.

"The Leighton boutique is on Bond Street," she stammered, caught in his gaze.

He gave a predatory smile. "My driver knows the way."

"Of course he does. You date so many women, I bet you go there a lot." She turned away, blinking fast as she stared out the window. Beneath her breath, she added wistfully, "It must be nice to never worry about money."

A sudden memory went through Maksim of the bone-chilling winter when he'd turned fourteen. There'd been no heat in their tiny apartment; his mother had been laid off from her temp job. Three-year-old Dariya had been shivering and crying, and their desperate mother had taken her to a shelter to get warm. Wanting to help, he'd cut school to sell newspapers on the street in Philadelphia. Freezing rain soaked through everything. It had taken three days afterward for Maksim's coat to dry—three days of winter so cold it left his skin the color of ash. Three days of a wet, icy wind that seeped beneath his clothes and left him shaking till his teeth chattered.

Three days of hiding the wet coat from his mother, knowing that she would insist on giving him her own, that she'd go without a coat herself as she trudged the distance between employment agencies, desperate to find a job, any job.

Those three days had taught him the most valuable lesson of his life.

Money made the difference between a good life and no life at all.

Money fixed anything. Money fixed everything.

And you didn't get it by being nice.

"What a fairy-tale life," the girl whispered, staring out the window at all the well-dressed shoppers on Bond Street, the expensive cars, the festive decorations and lights of Christmas. "A perfect fairy-tale life."

Looking at her wistful beauty, Maksim suddenly had the strong desire to tell this naive girl the truth about his ruthless soul.

But he didn't. She'd learn it soon enough.

She'd learn it the hard way.

Grace Cannon would tell Maksim what he needed to know. He would try to buy the information. If that didn't work, he'd seduce it from her.

Or maybe, he thought suddenly as he looked down at her, he would seduce her anyway.

He would show this little secretary a kind of romance she'd never seen before. Luxury on a grand scale. He would be lavish. He would kiss her senseless. And like every woman before her, she would fall.

He would make her talk.

He would take her body.

Then…he would drop her.

A man didn't get rich—or win—by being nice.

CHAPTER THREE

ELEGANT shops always made Grace uncomfortable, and the Leighton boutique was the snootiest shop on Bond Street.

She could feel herself tensing up the moment she walked through the door, past grim-jawed security guards in suits like FBI agents. They gave her a hard stare, and she had the sudden feeling they were waiting for her to make one false step so they could take her down as a warning to other broke secretaries who might try to venture inside this rarefied, exclusive world.

Grace swallowed, looking around the elegant primrose-colored boutique. Buying the lingerie the first time had just about killed her. Buying it on behalf of the man she loved, as a gift for another woman—in such a teensy, tiny size, to boot—was just another painful reminder of the fact that Alan had chosen Lady Francesca Danvers over her. The moment Alan had met the beautiful, wealthy aristocrat, he'd forgotten all about the drunken kiss he'd given Grace just the previous night.

It had been Grace's very first kiss. But for him it had been instantly forgettable.

"Back again, I see," the snooty salesgirl sniffed. She looked dismissively from Grace's worn, wet coat to her scuffed-up boots. "Here to do more Christmas shopping for your boss?"

"I, um, yes." She swallowed. "I need more lingerie. The same exact one. I lost—"

But as she spoke, the salesgirl's eyes moved over her shoulder as someone new entered the shop.

Grace didn't need to look around to know it was Maksim. She knew from the immediate electricity in the room. She knew from the thousand watts that lit up the salesgirl's face as she nearly knocked Grace over in her haste to cross the marble floor. Reaching toward him. Wanting him like every woman in London.

Every woman except *her,* Grace told herself. He was dangerous and handsome and powerful, and he was her enemy. She didn't want him. She *didn't.*

"Your Highness! Such a pleasure to see you again," the brunette cried. "We have plenty of new stock—I'd love to show it to you!"

It was painfully obvious to Grace what the salesgirl would really love to show Maksim. For no good reason she felt herself get tight and tense all over. She turned away, used to feeling invisible. In her job, on the street, living alone in a foreign country…invisible. Alone.

Then she felt a strong masculine hand on her shoulder.

"You will start by getting my beautiful friend a replacement of the lingerie she bought," Maksim said to the salesgirl. He looked down at Grace. "Then—you will get her anything else she desires in the store."

"Yes, of course, Your Highness," the salesgirl gasped, her mouth a round *O* as she looked at Grace with new respect.

His steel-gray eyes and the touch of his hand caused a flash of heat to spread through her body.

"I splashed you with my car," he said. "It was an unforgivable rudeness. The least I can do is buy you new clothes. A new coat."

Grace stared at him, warmth cascading all over her. A moment before, she'd felt so invisible and cold, but with one touch he made her feel alive. With one word he'd made her feel she had value in the world.

"Anything you want, Grace," he said softly, stroking her cheek. "Anything at all. It will be my deepest honor to provide."

A shudder of longing went through her. Her face turned involuntarily toward his touch, and his hand cupped her cheek. She tried to pull away from him, but her feet weren't working properly. Neither was the rest of her.

Except for her breasts which started to ache, sending sizzles of longing down to her deepest core.

And at that moment Grace started to realize how dangerous the dark prince truly was.

She licked her lips. "Thank you, but I couldn't possibly accept."

His hand traced lightly down her neck to her shoulder, to her coat. "Why do you hide in these clothes, Grace? Why are you afraid to show the world your beauty?"

He really thought she was pretty? It hadn't just been

flattery? Her mind was spinning a million directions at once, and as long as he kept touching her she couldn't think straight. "I—"

"This would look lovely on you."

He touched a lovely pink nightgown displayed on a white headless mannequin. The silk and lace were the blush color of a spring rose, and while the low-cut neckline was covered in lace, the rest of the fabric went elegantly to the floor.

Grace, who normally slept in T-shirts and flannel pants, couldn't imagine sleeping in anything so sybaritic and luxurious.

Against her will, her eyes traced the shape of Maksim's muscular fingers against the delicate silk. She had the sudden image of what it might feel like to be in that nightgown with his hands on her. To be touched and caressed and stroked through the silk by his strong, powerful touch.

Grace fiercely shook the evocative image out of her mind.

What was wrong with her? She was growing as headless as the mannequin! No man had ever seen her in nightwear. Not even in her flannel pajamas. And it was likely to remain so!

"I'm not in the habit of letting strangers buy me nightgowns," she said, pulling her hand away from him and forcibly turning her back on the lovely pink silk.

"No lingerie, then," he said, sounding amused. "In that case, a coat. This one?"

"A coat?" She turned around, tempted. In spite of the cashmere blanket and warmth of his car, she was still shivering from the melted sleet and slush seeping through her old camel-colored coat. Having never owned a proper coat in California, she'd bought this one at a charity shop in London. It had seemed serviceable enough, and the price had been right. But it didn't hold up very well to rain, and was terribly ugly in the bargain, though Grace tried not to care.

"My car splashed your coat. It's ruined," he pointed out. "Surely even your overheightened sense of honor would allow me to replace it as a matter of course."

He touched a truly beautiful ankle-length black shearling coat with a wide collar. It was a dazzling sight, fit for a princess. She'd admired the coat when she'd first come into the shop a few hours ago. But she'd only admired it from a distance—she hadn't been nearly brave enough to actually touch it. Particularly after her eye had fallen on the price tag. Ten thousand pounds. In dollars, that equaled—

A new car.

She closed her eyes, suppressing her desire.

"And you must have this, as well." He pointed at an exquisite silk cocktail dress. "The color matches your eyes."

She looked at it hungrily. The dress was beautiful—something out of the fashion magazines she saw on newsstands. She reached out to touch the silk, then at the last moment hesitated and took the price tag instead. Four thousand pounds.

What was she thinking? She couldn't allow her boss's rival to buy her even a cocktail, let alone a cocktail dress!

Clothes like these were for glamorous, beautiful heiresses like Lady Francesca. Not for broke, plain girls like her. She'd bought her boots at a discount warehouse. Her shirt had cost less than ten dollars at Wal-Mart, and she'd bought her skirt suit used at a consignment shop in Los Angeles. For the past five years, since her father had died, she'd scrimped everywhere she could to help her family.

A lump rose in her throat. But it still hadn't been enough. She never should have left her mother alone....

"Let me do this small thing for you," Maksim said decisively. "You cannot refuse me this pleasure."

And she almost couldn't. She almost didn't want to refuse him *any* pleasure.

But she couldn't accept. She didn't trust him. And as much as she wanted these beautiful luxuries, she knew they weren't for her. Nothing in the Leighton boutique related to real life!

"And just where do you think I would wear that dress?" she retorted, raising her chin so he wouldn't know how tempted her weak soul had been. "To the grocery store? The post office?"

His lips curved into a smile. "I can think of a few places you could wear it. And not wear it."

Immediately a shiver of longing went through her body at his sensual smile. Why was he acting like this, wooing her as if she were a desirable, demanding woman?

There could be only one reason the ruthless billionaire prince would have any interest in her: he wanted to use her to get back the things Alan had stolen.

The merger.

The bride.

Grace resolutely turned away. From him, from the black coat, from the extravagant teal cocktail dress and the lavish, hedonistic life they represented. She wouldn't sell herself, or sell out Alan.

"No," she said, forcing down the hunger in her soul for everything she knew she'd never have. "I'll allow you to replace the lingerie. No more."

He shrugged. "It's just money, Grace."

Just money. The words made her want to laugh. Easy enough to say just money when you had plenty of it. Just money had made Grace drop out of college when her father died five years ago. Just money had made her mother worry about bills ever since, with three teenaged sons who ate out the refrigerator daily. And just money was about to make her family lose the only home they'd ever known.

"What is it?" Maksim's steel-gray eyes were intent on hers, mesmerizing her will with the whispered promise of all her lost dreams. "Tell me what you want. Anything you desire, Grace. Say the word, and it is yours."

"A couple of mortgage payments," she said under her breath.

"What?"

"I...I...it's nothing." She couldn't possibly ask Alan's enemy for a loan. She could only guess what the cost could be. She'd have to stab Alan in the back. She wouldn't do that, not for any price.

Alan will advance me the money, she told herself desperately. *He will!*

With a deep intake of breath, she turned away from

Maksim to speak directly to the salesgirl. "Just the white silk-and-lace babydoll, please. Size extra small."

"I have it here, miss," the brunette said respectfully. Grace watched as the girl folded the lingerie carefully, then wrapped it in tissue paper. She placed it in a glossy primrose-hued box embossed with the Leighton crest, then tied it with a white silk ribbon.

"Only one woman in a hundred would have turned down my offer," the Russian prince said quietly from behind her. "One in a thousand."

She looked back at him with a trembling attempt at a smile. "You are my boss's rival. I feel enough of a traitor allowing you to replace the lingerie. Accepting a gift from you would not be appropriate."

"No one would ever know about it."

"I would know. And so would you."

"Ah." He looked down at her, his dark eyes intent. "A woman of honor."

She felt uncomfortable, unsure of what response to make. The way he looked at her didn't help. It just made her jumpy in her own skin. After feeling invisible for so long, being so suddenly *seen* by a man like Maksim made her dizzy.

It was like spending years in the darkness and then abruptly being hit by a blaze of sun. It sizzled her all over. She felt blinded by the intensity of his heat.

From the corner of her eye, she saw the salesgirl hold out the bag with a bright smile. "Merry Christmas, miss. Please come again soon."

"Allow me." Maksim took the bag, carrying it for her. A prince *and* a gentleman?

It shocked her. If she'd been shopping with Alan, he would have made her carry everything. He liked to keep his hands free. After all, he always joked, didn't women love to carry shopping bags? But then, Alan was her boss.

Maksim was…her enemy?

He was different from any man she'd ever known before. Dangerous. Because he was so handsome? Ruthless. Because he was a billionaire? And gallant. Because he was a prince?

Whatever it was, he was just like the Leighton clothes. Not for Grace. Nothing to do with real life. And yet she couldn't look away, and a part of her couldn't stop wondering what it would be like to be his woman.

As they climbed into his waiting Rolls-Royce, she felt the strength of his hand beneath her arm as he helped her in. Felt his touch up and down her body. And she trembled in her wet coat for reasons that had nothing to do with cold.

"Is it strange for you to buy lingerie for your ex-girlfriend?" she murmured as the car pulled away from the curb.

He shrugged, looked away. "She may someday be my girlfriend again."

"But she's engaged to Alan."

She saw the twitch in his jaw. "And two months ago she was with me."

"You can't possibly think—"

"I don't wish to speak of her." He took both her hands in his own. "I wish to speak only of you." He looked down at her and the edges of his lips turned up. "You need warming up."

"I…do?" she breathed.

"Join me for dinner tonight."

He was asking her out on a date? She tried not to tremble. Failed. "I couldn't possibly."

His dark eyebrows lowered. "Why?"

"I'm not hungry, for one." As if on cue, her stomach gave an audible growl and she blushed. She'd worked through lunch writing engagement announcements for Alan's friends and family, while her boss met Francesca for a celebratory lunch at her father's estate outside the city. "If Alan found out…"

"He won't."

"Splurging on dinner is not in my budget."

"I will of course be pleased to—"

"No."

He sighed, clearly exasperated. "You make it impossible to pamper you."

"I don't want you to pamper me." Her stomach growled again, and she bit her lip. "But…perhaps a small snack wouldn't hurt. As long as we go Dutch." *And as long as Alan never finds out.* "There's a tea shop by Harrods, close to our house."

He raised his eyebrows. "'Our' house?" he asked innocently. "You have a roommate?"

She felt a blush go across her cheeks. "I share a house with Alan."

He gave her a knowing glance. "I see."

"We're not lovers, if that's what you think!" But she could see he didn't believe her. She felt her cheeks turn redder still. "I have my own three-room flat in his basement. As his executive secretary, he needs me to always be available. With London rents as expensive as they are, I'm happy to have a place to stay."

"How very convenient for you both," he murmured silkily.

"You don't understand," she stammered. "It's all fair and aboveboard. He deducts the cost of the rent from my salary each month!"

He suddenly laughed. "Does he really? So you're available to him around the clock, running his personal errands on your own time…and he still makes you pay money to live in his basement?" He shook his head. "I can see why he inspires such loyalty."

"Oh, forget it," she said in a huff, sitting back against the seat and staring stonily out at passing Hyde Park. "If you're going to insult Alan, you can forget the tea and just take me home."

"I didn't insult him."

"You did!"

"I'm just surprised at your loyalty. You deserve more."

She stared at him. She deserved more? It was an entirely new thought. She'd spent three years in low-paying temp jobs in downtown L.A. before she'd been hired by Cali-West. She'd been instantly smitten by the powerful, blond, handsome CEO who looked like a young Hugh Grant. She'd thought herself very lucky.

But the darkly handsome Russian prince thought she deserved…more?

"Are we close to the tea shop?" Maksim asked. She saw the driver waiting for directions, glancing at her in the rearview mirror.

She pointed grumpily. "Right there. Just past the light."

The white-haired lady who owned the patisserie appeared flustered by Maksim's broad-shouldered form appearing in the doorway of her dainty shop. He seemed massively masculine, out of place against the faded flowery wallpaper. She immediately seated them at the best table, tucked in a corner window overlooking the crowds and festive windows of Harrods across the street. When the Frenchwoman asked for their order, Grace waited for Maksim to order first, as Alan would have done.

Instead, he looked at her questioningly, reaching across the small table to take her hand. "What do you recommend, Grace?"

"I...um." She glanced down at her hand wrapped in his far larger one. She could barely think with him touching her. "The...er..." She pulled her hand away under pretense of picking up the gently tattered menu that she'd long ago learned by heart. "The English breakfast tea is good. The pastries are excellent, and so are the sandwiches." She looked up at Madame Charbon, handing back her menu. "I'll have my usual."

The woman nodded.

Maksim handed her his menu. "I'll have the same."

"Oui, monsieur."

As the Frenchwoman departed, Grace looked at him in surprise. "You don't even know what you just ordered!"

He shrugged. "You know this restaurant. I trust you."

He trusted her. She tried not to feel flattered. "Want to know what you're having?"

"I like surprises."

Normally Grace didn't, but she was starting to. She

took a deep breath. "I'm sorry I was so upset in the car. I guess you really weren't insulting Alan."

"He is lucky to have you."

She stared down at the tiny table. The truth was it was sometimes grating how small her paycheck was. And never more so than now. She'd been his junior secretary for eighteen months before she was promoted to executive assistant six months ago. But in spite of her additional responsibilities, he'd never given her a raise commensurate with her new position. He'd always managed to put her off with an excuse and a smile.

Then he'd decided to pursue a long-shot merger with Exemplary Oil PLC and he'd abruptly moved them to London in early October. In L.A. Grace had had fewer expenses. She'd been able to live at home and help her family. Now that she lived in London and paid Alan rent, she was barely able to send her mother a hundred dollars a month.

This led to one inescapable conclusion: the looming foreclosure of her family's home was entirely Grace's fault.

As Madame Charbon arrived with the steaming mugs of hot chocolate and croissants, Grace tried to push the depressing thoughts away. They just made her feel more powerless and scared and…angry.

Alan will help me. He will, she repeated to herself.

"What are you thinking about, *solnishka mayo?*" Maksim asked, leaning forward as he looked at her keenly.

She gulped down some hot chocolate, scalding her tongue. "Nothing. Um. I was just wondering if you've ever ridden the Trans-Siberian Railroad."

His dark eyebrows rose. "An odd question."

"You're Russian, aren't you?" She smiled wistfully. "I used to dream about that train when I was a little girl, a train that crosses seven time zones and nearly six thousand miles, going all the way from Moscow to the Pacific Ocean."

"Sorry to disappoint you," he said dryly. "I live in Moscow only a few months a year. When I travel or visit the northern oil fields I go by jet."

"Of course you do," she said with a sigh. "So where do you live when you're not in Russia? London?"

"I have many houses around the world. Six or seven. I live in whichever one is convenient."

She stared at him. "Six or seven? You're not even sure how many?"

He shrugged. "I have as many as I need. I sell them when I'm bored." He licked the thick whipped cream off the top of the mug with his wide tongue, causing her to stare in spite of herself. He took a sip of hot chocolate, then a bite of the croissant. "This is delicious."

"I'm glad you like it. Alan hates hot chocolate."

Maksim's eyes suddenly sliced through hers. "You're in love with him, aren't you?"

She felt sucker punched.

"What?" she whispered. "Who?"

"You're his loyal slave. You live in his house. You spend your free hours running his errands. It's plain you're not doing it for the money, since you have none. There's only one explanation. You love him."

Grace opened up her mouth to deny it, but suddenly she was so tired of lying. Tired of holding everything inside, of keeping it together, of having no one to confide in and no one she could rely upon. She took a deep breath.

"Yes. I love him." Sinking her head into her hands, she whispered, "It's hopeless."

"I know." She looked up, saw surprising warmth and sympathy in his handsome face. "I'm usually on the other side of it. Old or young, secretaries imagine themselves in love with me and drop like flies from my office. It's painful. It causes disruption. I hate it."

"Me, too." She gave a little laugh that ended with a sob—or was it a sob that ended with a laugh? She tried her best at a laissez-faire shrug. "And now he's engaged to someone who's beautiful, wealthy and so, well…"

"Vicious?" His eyes met hers. "Cruel and mean?"

With a gulp, she nodded. "I'm surprised to hear you say that. Didn't you love her?"

He changed the subject. "You don't have to endure it, Grace. Come work for me instead."

It was a good thing she'd already finished her hot chocolate or it would have snorted out her nose. Her eyes flew open, and she saw he wasn't joking. He was deadly serious.

Her throat closed.

"Work for you?" she gasped.

"I could use another secretary. Leave Barrington. Work for a man who will pay you well and take you far." He smiled. "The fact that you're in love with someone else is actually in your favor."

She swallowed. "Even though it's the man who stole your girlfriend?"

He took another drink of the hot chocolate.

"Delicious," he murmured, then looked up at her. "I need a secretary I can trust, Grace. A smart woman who knows the meaning of loyalty. You wouldn't regret changing your allegiance. I swear to you."

For an instant she was tempted. What would it be like to work for this handsome prince, instead of Alan?

Maksim was handsome, dangerous and ruthless. But he was also a man she would be free to fight, free to leave, free to speak her mind with, because she did not love him!

"I would pay you double whatever Barrington's paying you."

Double?

She licked her lips. "Would you consider paying me in advance?"

He didn't even hesitate. "Yes."

She took a deep breath, tempted beyond measure. This could save her mother's house. Save everything.

"And the catch?"

"You would help me win the merger."

"And Francesca?"

He shrugged, then held out his hand. "Do we have a deal?"

Grace closed her eyes, remembering all the times Alan had teased her, flirted with her. He'd told her more than once that he never wanted her to leave him. "I just couldn't survive without you, Gracie," he'd said with his charming movie-star grin. And it had made her so happy! She'd hugged his words to her heart, hoping that he might be starting to see her as more than just a secretary!

Then Lady Francesca Danvers had offered him money and power in such a perfectly beautiful package.

But no matter how Alan had treated her, Grace couldn't betray him.

Stubborn and foolish, she thought sourly, but she shook her head. "Thanks for asking, but my answer is no."

Taking back his hand, he nodded. "I understand."

But he didn't seem disappointed. On the contrary, he seemed to savor her refusal like a cat licking a bowl of cream.

Finishing the last crumbs of her croissant, Grace left some coins on the table and rose regretfully from her chair. She held out her hand.

"Thank you for a very pleasant afternoon, Prince Maksim."

He looked at her, and for a moment she was lost in his gaze, swirling in the endless shades of gray.

"No. I thank you, Grace." He took her hand in his own. A sizzling warmth spread through her body from their intertwined fingers. Then, still holding her hand, he kissed each of her fingers, and she shivered.

"Da svedanya, solnishka mayo. I'll never forget the way you looked in the street, with the last rays of winter twilight in your pale-blond hair. Like an angel. Like the sun." He turned her hand over and kissed her palm. An erotic charge arced through her, making her nipples tight and her breasts heavy. Her whole body was suddenly tense, waiting, waiting...

Looking up into her face, he murmured, "Until we meet again."

He released her, and Grace walked out of the tea

shop in a daze. As she slogged through the crowds outside Harrods, gripping her Leighton bag as if her life depended on it, she could still feel that sensual kiss against her palm.

With one brief touch of his lips, he'd branded her. In the dark winter night lit up by Christmas lights and shop windows, she looked down at her right hand, expecting to see the burn of his lips emblazoned on her skin for all the world to see.

But her skin was bare.

She knew she'd never see him again. Probably a good thing.

Definitely a good thing.

And yet…

When Alan yelled at her for not magically foreseeing his wishes in advance…when a check bounced in her bank account…when she was forced to watch the man she loved get married to another woman…when she felt helpless, hopeless, invisible…

She could treasure this one magical afternoon when she'd spent the day with a handsome prince who'd been kind to her. Who'd treated her like a princess.

As she walked home, the sleet softened to snow in the dark stillness of winter, leaving scattered, twisted flurries of flakes.

She'd loved Alan Barrington in hopeless silence for two years. But he'd never affected her like Maksim Rostov had. He'd never made her tremble and shake and feel hot all over. Maksim had changed her in a way she couldn't understand.

But whatever he'd made her feel didn't matter now.

With a sigh that created a puff of white smoke in the frozen air, Grace climbed slowly up the front steps of the three-story town house she shared with her boss.

The fairy tale was over.

CHAPTER FOUR

ALAN was waiting for her at the door with twinkling blue eyes. He was so boyishly handsome, he could almost be called pretty. Beaming with excitement, he dragged her into his reception room.

"You got home just in time, Gracie! I have a present for you!"

He placed a plane ticket into her hands. She stared down at it, and the sparkling white lights of his elegantly decorated Christmas tree seemed to whirl around her in the front room of his Knightsbridge town house.

"Merry Christmas," he purred.

Sucking in her breath, she looked up at him. And to think she'd wondered in her darker moments if he intentionally used her own feelings against her, taking advantage of her crush to avoid having to properly pay her. But with this gift, there could be no doubt that he truly cared for her...otherwise, why would he have done this?

"Thank you," she whispered. "I wanted so much to go home for Christmas. But I didn't have enough to—"

"I know, Gracie," he said with a big smile.

"Thank you, Alan," she said, feeling as if she was going to cry. "This means so much to me."

"On Christmas Eve, as soon as the deal is finished, you'll fly off to enjoy the sun and surf." He sighed. "I don't know how I'll survive while you're gone."

She took a deep breath. "Alan, I have a really big favor to ask you—"

"Oh, no." He groaned. "Not the raise again. Does it always have to be about money? I'm the CEO of Cali-West and you're my righthand woman." He gave her a wink. "Isn't that glory enough for you?"

His righthand woman, but not the woman in his arms. Grace managed a weak smile. "You said we could talk about maybe a raise or bonus at the end of the year, and I'm really desperate, Alan, because—"

"Sorry, kiddo." He held up his hand. "That'll have to wait a bit longer. I'm late for my date with Francesca."

"But Alan—"

"We'll talk about it tomorrow. I really promise this time." He took her hand, and she felt nothing like the painful zing she'd experienced with Maksim. Alan's hand was just warm and soft. "In the meantime, there's something I need you to do for me. A teensy, small favor." He flashed her a big white grin. "Help me get married."

"Wh-what?"

"Francesca's having trouble setting the wedding date. So I thought—why bother with a wedding at all? Why not just elope? That's where you come in." He gave her a bright smile. "Christmas Eve I want to elope. Scotland. Honeymoon in Barbados. I need you to make the arrangements."

Alan didn't realize what he was asking of her. How could he? To him, Halloween night had been just a kiss. To her, it had been the culmination of two years of fantasies. Which was probably why the kiss hadn't felt nearly as intense as she'd imagined it would. Not even as intense as the way Prince Maksim's lips had felt against her palm an hour before.

Trying to push the memory of the dark Russian prince from her mind, she took a deep breath. "Are you sure eloping is a good idea? The bride might prefer to choose when—"

"It's perfect," he said, frowning.

"All right," she sighed. She suddenly realized she was still clutching the Leighton bag in her hands. "Here's your gift."

"Thanks." Taking his coat from the hall closet, he slung the bag over his shoulder. He stopped at the door with a wink. "I'll need this tonight to close the deal. I'll be getting her something better for Christmas. In the meantime, start working on the elopement plans, will you?"

After Grace locked the door behind him, she turned back with a lump in her throat.

She'd thought buying gifts for his fiancée was bad. Planning their quickie wedding would be a thousand times worse.

It hurt more than she'd expected.

Because she'd spent the afternoon with Prince Maksim, she realized. Because for the first time in years she'd felt the full attention of a man's eyes on her, the consideration of his touch and regard, and it had brought something to life inside her. Something that wanted to be seen. Something that wanted to be touched. It had felt so good. She'd felt…

Alive.

Now she just felt numb.

Grace went downstairs to her basement apartment. Closing the door quietly behind her, she changed out of her damp clothes. She put on an old sweatshirt and flannel pajama pants. She heated some leftover takeaway Thai food in her microwave. She sat down heavily on the couch. She turned on the old television. She placed a fork, the food and a diet soda on the coffee table. She got out her laptop to start making elopement arrangements for Christmas Eve, just two weeks away.

But instead of opening her laptop or watching TV, she wrapped herself in the quilt her mother had made her as a child. She sat on the couch and stared blankly at the wall.

He was really going to marry Lady Francesca Danvers. The vicious, skinny, gorgeous heiress who always got away with her bad behavior because she was so beautiful that men put up with it. Men would put up with anything to be with a girl like that.

While Grace was such a pushover she couldn't even make Alan listen to her beg him for an advance. Not even though her family's security depended on it.

Tears fell softly onto the frayed fabric of the quilt. Why hadn't she found out until that morning that her father's life insurance money was gone? Why hadn't she known her mother had been keeping their financial difficulties secret? And why couldn't she stop loving a man who so plainly saw her as nothing but a secretary?

She jumped when she heard a loud knock at her front door.

Fiercely wiping her eyes, she wrapped her mother's quilt over her shoulders and rose from the couch. Alan had likely forgotten his key again and wanted to go up through her apartment. Her nervous heart beat faster. This time she would make him listen. *I need an advance,* she practiced in her mind. *Please, Alan, I need $10,000 right away or my family will lose their home.*

She opened the door into the dark, snowy night. "Alan, I need—"

Her words ended in a gasp.

The tall, dark-haired man who looked down at her with a gleam in his eye was definitely *not* her boss.

Prince Maksim leaned against the edge of the door, looking dangerous and oh, so seductive in a tuxedo beneath a black coat. Her heart pounded in a whole new way.

"What are you doing here?" she breathed.

"I forgot something," he said, looking down at her tear-stained face.

"What?"

She caught a sudden brief blur of icy moonlight above as she felt his hands, his warmth, wrapping around her. Saw the colors of her quilt blur around her as he cupped her face.

"This," he said simply.

And he kissed her.

The touch of Maksim's mouth on hers was gentle at first. He pulled her close. She felt his hands brush through her hair before they moved slowly down her back. Her breasts pressed against his hard chest. He held her more tightly, deepening the embrace. His lips caressed hers, leading her, teaching her, making her sizzle all the way to her toes. He forced her lips wide, penetrating her mouth, teasing and licking her with the tip of his tongue. Her whole body became tight with longing, and her core poured with heat.

It was the kiss she'd always dreamed of. The whole world seemed to whirl and shudder around her like a tornado as she was swept up in his fierce embrace.

Was she dreaming? She had to be dreaming!

Feeling Maksim's strong arms around her, his lips taking his pleasure and demanding she take her own, was like nothing she'd ever felt before. Nothing like Alan's sloppy, drunken kiss six weeks earlier.

Alan!

She was kissing Alan's enemy in his own house!

"Stop," she whimpered against his lips, shuddering as she pulled away. "Please stop."

He pushed blond tendrils from her face. "Because you're in love with Barrington?"

"No…yes." She shook her head with a tearful laugh. "You just have to go!"

"You just have to come with me."

He wanted her to go out with him? "I don't need your pity—"

"Pity?" His eyes darkened until they were almost black in the snowy, cloud-ribboned moonlit night. "I have been accused of having no heart. I am telling you the truth, Grace. Take this as a warning."

And he kissed her again.

This time he was not gentle. It was a hard plundering of her mouth that bruised her lips and left her dizzy, aching with pleasure.

"Come out with me tonight," he whispered against her cheek. "You cannot refuse me."

Though she'd been standing for five minutes in the below-street-level entrance of her basement flat, she was barely aware of the cold.

But how could she be tempted? She loved Alan!

Didn't she?

"I won't turn on him," she gasped, still trembling with the shock of desire. "Not for any price. You won't kiss a betrayal out of me."

"You think that's the only reason I would kiss you?" The rich moonlight moved against scattered dark clouds above them, wistful and haunted, tracing his razor-sharp cheekbones and chiseled jaw. "You are a desirable woman, *solnishka mayo.*"

"Solnishka mayo?" she repeated.

"Sunlight," he whispered.

She choked out a laugh, glancing down at her flannel pajama pants, her ratty sweatshirt. She pulled her mother's quilt a little tighter over her shoulders. "You're blind."

"You don't know your own beauty." He stroked her shoulder, running his hand down the quilt as he looked down into her eyes, towering over her. "Let me show you the truth."

"But I can't trust you," she whispered. Prince Maksim was dangerous and ruthless. Though knowing he was forbidden to her just made her want him more....

He leaned down to kiss one cheek softly, then the other, as he spoke against her skin. "I'm not leaving without you."

The touch of his lips against her cheek sent aching tension to her breasts and down deep in her belly. She longed for him to kiss her again. In his arms she couldn't think, she couldn't do anything but feel. She closed her eyes as she felt his hot breath against the tender flesh of her ear. "I…I can't."

"You can and you will," he said. "Let me show you how pleasurable life can be."

With those words he pulled away from her. She nearly protested aloud and her eyelids reluctantly fluttered open. He was at least six inches taller than her, making her feel delicate. "No."

"Stubborn and foolish," he repeated softly, rubbing his thumb lightly against her swollen lower lip. "Why do you resist me?"

"Because…because…" She couldn't think straight with him stroking her lip like that. Grace's whole body ached. "I…don't have anything to wear."

With a sudden grin, he snapped his fingers. A bodyguard—a dark, hulking man who had to weigh three hundred pounds—ambled down the steps to her basement door with two primrose boxes in his arms. He set them near the doorway, then disappeared back up to the street.

An exclamation of shock escaped Grace as she stared at the two recognizably colored boxes embossed with the Leighton coat of arms.

"What have you done?"

"The coat," he said. "The dress."

She licked her lips. "Not the ones from Leighton."

"I knew you wanted them, though you denied it."

Remembering how she'd yearned for the black coat and the teal silk cocktail gown, a shiver swept through her body. She'd been afraid to even touch them in the store. At the thought of wearing them against her skin, her heart pounded.

He's luring me, she warned herself desperately. *Luring me to my own destruction!*

"I guessed your size, but have others in the car if necessary." His eyes met hers. "Women's clothes have always been a mystery to me. I've always been more interested in taking them off."

She gave an involuntary shiver. Then she looked down at the boxes, licking her lips, torn with longing.

He grabbed her wrist.

"Fair warning, Grace," he said quietly. "I will seduce you tonight."

Caught in his gaze, she couldn't breathe. Her heart almost felt about ready to explode from her chest.

"You're welcome to try," she managed over the rapid pounding of her heart. "I will resist you."

He gave her a slow, seductive smile. "I would expect nothing less."

She looked at the Leighton boxes. "And I can't... won't...accept expensive gifts."

"They weren't expensive."

"I saw one of the price tags in the boutique. The coat alone cost ten thousand pounds."

"You are worth far more than that." He stroked her

cheek. "I would pay any price to give you pleasure. Any price to please you."

The reminder of his wealth and power made her tremble. The money that felt like nothing to him was a fortune to her. More than enough to save her family. She closed her eyes. No. She wouldn't think about it. Asking Alan's enemy for help would blacken her soul beyond recognition. She might be weak, but she wasn't a traitor.

"If Alan found out I went out with you, he'd fire me."

"In which case you could come work for me," he said.

"But—"

"Either wear these clothes or go naked." He gave her a slow-rising smile. "Decide. Or I will."

Without asking permission, he pushed past her into her flat, carrying the boxes and pulling Grace behind him. He closed the door. They were alone.

The air seemed to leave the small apartment.

Prince Maksim Rostov—in her flat? She saw him look around at her sagging, plaid, threadbare couch. The day-old Thai takeout in the cardboard container. The blaring television with faded stars sparkling in sequins dancing to ballroom music. The laptop computer set up by her couch. Her cheeks burned.

He turned to her with a sensual smile. "Or we could just stay in."

Stay here—with him?

Ohmygodohmygod. *No.*

"The dress and coat would have to be a loan," she heard herself whisper. "I would give them back to you at the end of the night."

He smiled down at her.

"I'll look forward to it."

A dark force in his eyes pulled her with all the force of gravity. He looked at her as if he'd already undressed her and tossed her naked into his bed.

Bed? Who was thinking about bed?

Going out with him tonight, she was risking everything for a dangerous feeling she couldn't control. But she suddenly hungered to feel something that wasn't grief, loneliness or fear. She wanted to forget. She wanted to disappear into another world.

Her knees shook as she gathered up the boxes. "I'll be right back."

"I'll be waiting."

She hurried to her tiny bedroom, feeling strangely lighthearted. She brushed out her blond hair for two minutes with a hair dryer, then dabbed on some lipstick. She had no bra that would work with the cocktail dress, so she left her breasts bare beneath the dress. As she pulled the aquamarine gown over her hips, the softness of the luxurious silk slid like the whisper of a caress.

She knew she shouldn't do this.

Just one night, she told herself. *One night to forget my problems. I won't let him seduce me.*

She glanced at herself in the mirror and nearly gasped. She looked nothing like the downtrodden, damp, dowdy secretary she'd been just a few moments before. Aside from her old shoes, the scuffed silver pumps which were her only option, she almost didn't recognize herself. Who was the blond, bright-eyed young woman in the mirror?

The teal silk exactly matched the shade of her eyes.

The rose-pink lipstick made her pale skin look creamy. The cut of the gown made her full breasts look exactly right with her small waist, giving her the hourglass shape of a 1950s pinup girl.

Could clothes and makeup really do so much?

It wasn't just the clothes, she realized. It was *him*. His attention was making her blossom like a flower.

One night, she repeated to herself, and her teeth chattered. Just a few hours to feel pretty. She wouldn't let him seduce her. She couldn't. She was in love with someone else, which meant she was perfectly safe. Right?

Coming out of the bedroom, she stopped abruptly when she saw him leaning against the wall of the hallway. Maksim was so dark and handsome and terrifying. His gaze held her own, electrifying her.

"Sorry to make you wait," she said.

He came forward, stalking her like a jungle cat. He looked slowly over her body, from the blue-green silk skimming her curves to the silver drops dangling from her ears, from her long, thick blond hair to her full pink lips. He gave a long, slow whistle.

"You, *solnishka mayo,*" he said in a low voice, "were utterly worth waiting for."

CHAPTER FIVE

As THE chauffeur drove through the London streets, Grace watched feather-edged moonlight from the window move over Maksim's sharp cheekbones, his angular jawline. He was the most beautiful man she'd ever seen.

Beautiful. A strange word to describe such a powerful, dangerous man. But he *was* beautiful—hauntingly so. The moonlight caressed his straight nose, the cleft of his hard jaw, the hinted strength and latent brutality of the muscular body beneath the tuxedo and black coat.

He turned to meet her eyes, and his gaze scorched her, his gray eyes like smoke twisting from a deep hidden fire.

Grace suddenly realized…he hadn't lied. *He did want her.*

Innocent as she was, she could feel it.

He wasn't showing pity—or even kindness.

He wanted her.

The Leighton clothes had somehow transformed her into a beautiful, desirable woman. She'd felt downtrodden and invisible—now she felt like a goddess. Or possibly a sex kitten. An answering fire burned inside her with his every touch, every hot glance.

It wouldn't last. Like Cinderella's, her dress would disappear at the end of the night. She couldn't keep these things. She wouldn't let him buy her. She wouldn't let him seduce her.

But…for this one night, she could be the woman these clothes had created. She would have one night of magic. One night to be *seen*.

She would be the princess in the fairy tale.

The limo pulled smoothly to a stop at the curb. Maksim got out of the car and opened her door himself. Holding her arm in his own, steadying her on the icy sidewalk beneath the softly falling snow, he led her down a popular Covent Garden street filled with pubs and restaurants. Her black shearling coat swished against her ankles as she walked. Between the coat and Maksim's hand on hers, she felt warm in the frozen winter air.

"This way." He led her into a stately Victorian building, through a hidden door beside a chic tavern. She saw an elegant foyer, complete with a crystal chandelier, a front desk concierge and a security guard.

"Where are we going?"

"The top two floors of this building were converted into a penthouse." He gave her a brief smile. "A loft."

She stopped dead on the marble floor. "I'm not going to spend the evening alone with you at your house!"

"I don't live here. My sister does." He gave a careless shrug as he led her into a gilded elevator. "It's a bit colorful for my taste."

"So why did you buy it?"

Pressing on the elevator button, he looked down at her. "The Sheikh of Ramdah thought he could steal a pipeline deal from me. Instead I took his company and his favorite home in the bargain. To teach him a lesson."

The coldness in his voice made her shiver even more. "That's a bit ruthless, isn't it?" she ventured.

He gave a grim smile. "I protect what is mine."

When they arrived at the top floor, he knocked on the door. A ponderous, stiffly formal butler opened it to welcome them. His eyes widened. "Your Highness!"

"Oh!" A beautiful black-haired girl suddenly pushed past the butler to fling herself into Maksim's arms. "You're here! I can't believe you're here!"

He hugged her awkwardly, then drew back. "I wouldn't miss my own sister's birthday party."

"Liar," the girl said with a laugh. "You've missed the last two! And don't think expensive gifts make up for your absence. I don't need another Aston-Martin convertible, I need a brother—" She saw Grace and drew back in surprise. "But who's this?"

"A friend," he said.

"Funny, you've never bothered bringing 'friends' around before." She looked at Grace inquisitively, then pulled them both inside. "But I'm being rude. Come in! Come in!"

As the butler took their coats, the girl turned her piercing gray eyes, so much like her brother's, on Grace. "I'm Dariya Rostova."

Of course Grace knew the famous Princess Dariya, the fun-loving party girl who was constantly in the papers with her gorgeous friends. Pale and model slender in her silver sequin minidress, she wore a diamond tiara in her straight black hair.

Beneath her examination, Grace felt shy and out of place. "I'm sorry, I didn't know we were going to a birthday party," she stammered. "I'm afraid I don't have a gift."

Dariya suddenly smiled, and her lovely face lit up with warmth. "It wouldn't have even occurred to Francesca to bring a gift, so I already like you loads better. If you ask me, that woman was a snooty dry stick draped in furs."

"Dariya," her brother warned.

"What's your name?" his sister said, ignoring him.

She cleared her throat. "Grace."

"Well, Grace, you've actually brought the best present of the night." She beamed up at her brother fondly. "Come say hello to everyone!"

Dariya led them into the enormous loft, with soaringly high ceilings and big windows overlooking St. Martin's Lane. In the center of the room, a sharp, metallic chandelier held multicolored orbs for lights. Amid the vast space of the open-walled apartment, the furniture was a cross between 1960s retro and cartoonish avant-garde. Grace looked with dismay at backless chairs that were shaped like ripe strawberries.

"Look everyone," Dariya announced happily. "Look who came! And he even brought a friend. Everyone, say hello to Grace!"

As a cheer of welcome went around the room, Grace felt happy in a way she hadn't felt for months. She suddenly realized how much she'd missed having friends. She hadn't kept up with her old friends since she'd started working for Alan, much less tried to make new ones. She'd given up the idea of friends or hobbies or anything but being Alan's perfect on-call secretary.

But now…

The laughing, friendly group around her reminded Grace of bonfires on the beach when she'd been in school, before her father had died. Before she'd started working for Alan. Back when her life had been simple and easy. She ached remembering the fun she'd had, getting together with friends to eat, drink, talk and laugh.

The only difference being that these people were all impossibly rich and good-looking. And that the party was in an artistic, soaring two-floor loft that had once been the treasured possession of the Sheikh of Ramdah.

"I told you Maksim would come!" Dariya said triumphantly to a young man hovering nearby. "You owe me ten pounds!"

"Best bet I've ever lost. Hello, Maksim. Lovely to meet you, Grace," he said with a grin. "Thanks for putting a smile on my girl's face."

"*Your* girl?" Dariya tossed her dark hair. "In your dreams, Simon!"

Maksim growled something incomprehensible to the aristocratic young man. He was obviously being protective, but it still seemed rude. Grace cleared her throat and turned to Dariya. "So it's your twenty-fifth birthday?"

"Don't remind me," she groaned. She suddenly looked alarmed, putting her hands on her perfect face. "Do I look it?"

Grace laughed, then pointed at the hand-painted banner slung from the high, frescoed ceiling that read, *Happy Twenty-fifth Birthday, Dariya!* It was a charming homemade touch amid all the exorbitantly expensive, bright, sharp modernity.

"Oh. Right." The girl followed her glance with a sigh. "A quarter of a century, and what have I done with my life?"

"I just turned twenty-five on Sunday," Grace said sympathetically, "and I spent the day huddled in my flat in total denial."

"No, really!" Dariya exclaimed. "Not even a party?"

"My boss gave me a gift card for a week's worth of lunches at my favorite Japanese restaurant."

"You had no party," the girl repeated, shaking her head in horror. "You simply can't turn twenty-five without a party! Maksim," she turned to her brother, "tell her it's ridiculous!"

"Ridiculous," he agreed laconically.

"Lulu," Dariya called over her shoulder, "get a party hat, will you? Right. So this party will be for both of us." When Lulu brought the colorfully decorated hat, Dariya took the tiara off her head and stuck the hat in its place. "This will be for me." She placed the diamond tiara on Grace's blond head. "And that will be for you."

"Oh no," Grace gasped, feeling the weight of the diamonds on her head. She'd come without a gift, and now she was going to upstage Maksim's sister, the famous socialite Princess Dariya, during her own birthday party? "That's so generous of you, really, but I couldn't—"

"To be honest, it suits you better." She leaned forward and whispered mischievously in Grace's ear, "It was a gift from my brother, anyway, and not at all my style!"

"Dariya, you promised to dance!" Simon called from the other side of the loft, where a four-person jazz band had started to play.

"In a mo!" She gave Grace one last hug. "Must go dance, I'm afraid. Otherwise he'll pout, but I'm so glad you're here. My brother looks happy. Make yourself at home!"

After she left, Grace touched the top of her head. Was it possible that they were actually real diamonds? The thought shocked her…frightened her. The wealth around her was already far beyond anything she'd ever seen, even working as Alan's secretary. She felt like Alice who'd just stepped through the looking glass to a world where money really did grow on trees. And the tree branches were made of gold. And the berries were all diamonds, rubies and emeralds.

She felt Maksim come up behind her. Wrapping his arms around her, he kissed the crook of her neck. Her nipples instantly went hard, her breath shallow, her mind went dizzy. Then he whirled her around, handing her one of the crystal flutes from his other hand.

She took it with an awkward attempt at a smile. "My first champagne."

"Cristal is not a poor way to start."

She took a sip. The bubbles floated inside her, all soft and lovely and warm going down.

Maksim tilted her head upward with his hand, looking down at her from his towering height. His gaze was dark and intense. She suddenly knew he meant to kiss her again and she couldn't think. Couldn't even breathe.

Everything about him tempted her. Transfixed her. Made her long to really and truly be the woman who could mesmerize him in equal measure.

When would he kiss her?

Kiss her? What was she thinking? Clearly the tiara had constricted the blood flow to her brain!

Nervously she pulled away. She gulped down the rest of the expensive champagne as if chugging a can of soda, then pushed the tiara back crookedly on her head. "This thing isn't real, is it? The tiara's not real diamonds?"

He took a drink of champagne, his dark eyes resting on hers. "Set in platinum."

She swallowed, thinking that she likely could pay off her mother's whole mortgage with the sparkling tiara on her head. And maybe their neighbor's house in the bargain!

"What if I break it?" She gave a weak laugh. "Do you have insurance?"

"Diamonds don't break." Finishing his champagne, he took both flutes and set them on the tray of a passing waiter. He took her in his arms. "The tiara suits you. You should keep it." He slowly lowered his mouth toward hers. "You were born to wear jewels, Grace," he whispered. "Born to be adored and pampered in a life of luxury."

Someone turned out the side lights, leaving the loft lit only by the multicolored globes of the steel chandelier high above. Wide spotlights of red, green and blue shimmered in the semidarkness. In the wide space, she was aware of other people dancing, laughing, swaying to the music. She was in some strange fantastic world of stylish art, youth and limitless wealth.

But it wasn't the luxury that lured her most.

It was Maksim.

"I won't let you seduce me," she whispered, trying to reassure herself. "I won't."

Every inch of her body, down to blood and bone, ached for him to kiss her. Her body arched toward his, taut with longing as her teal silk dress slid like a whisper against his tuxedo.

Pulling her against his hard body, too arrogant to care who might be watching, he lowered his mouth to hers.

He kissed her so deeply that their tongues intertwined, kissed her so hard that with one embrace he bruised and branded her forever as his own.

No! She sagged against his chest, her heart pounding wildly when he released her from the kiss. She couldn't belong to Maksim. She couldn't!

He straightened the diamond tiara, stroking the long hair that brushed her bare shoulders, making her shiver. He took two more flutes of champagne from a passing tray. Then, taking her hand, he led her to the dance floor.

For the next few hours they drank champagne and danced together, their bodies swaying to the music. Time moved strangely, sliding sideways so hours felt like minutes, and minutes felt like eternity. They danced to the soulful jazz music, to the poignant cry of the saxophone, until finally he pulled her gently to the furthest side of the loft.

There, alone in the shadows and away from the others, he pushed her against the wall. He gently bit at her neck, sucking on her ear. She gasped, breathless and desperate for more.

He finally kissed her mouth, his tongue stroking hers deeply, luring her. And suddenly she could barely remember Alan's name, let alone why she should be loyal to him.

"Grace," Maksim murmured between kisses. "It's time to go."

"Go? Already?" she faltered.

"It's past midnight."

"Oh." And like Cinderella, that meant her time was up. The dream was over. She swallowed. "All right. I have a lot of work to do tomorrow, anyway."

"Then you'll be tired." He held her close, so close she could hear the beat of his heart. "I'm taking you to my hotel."

Hotel? A hard shiver racked her body.

"Come with me now," he whispered. "I can wait no longer. I want you in my bed."

She sucked in her breath, staring up into his eyes, caught by his dark, commanding gaze. She'd somehow wandered into a fairy-tale world, a place beyond her comprehension. She'd been drawn from the real world to become a princess in diamonds and teal silk, enslaved by a fantasy prince who compelled her to follow her deepest desires.

He was so handsome, she thought in a daze. Brutally masculine, like a sixteenth-century barbarian warlord. A dark czar from a mist-shrouded medieval age.

"Can you walk," he asked in a low voice, "or should I carry you?"

Walk? Her knees felt weak, whether from champagne or desire she wasn't sure. She glanced down at feet, at the cheaply made silver pumps, scuffed up at the toes, that she'd bought for fifteen dollars at a discount warehouse in Los Angeles. The shoes threatened to break the spell.

He led her from the dance floor. As he said their farewells to Dariya and her friends, Grace could barely speak as she looked up at Maksim.

He intended to take her to his hotel.

Could she resist?

Did she still even want to?

Maksim put her coat over her shoulders, pulling her close to button it up. She felt every brush of his fingertips like an earthquake through her body. He led her back to the elevator. Suddenly they were alone, and she trembled.

"Do you swear," she whispered, "seducing me isn't some backhanded way to hurt Alan?"

He put his hands on her shoulders and looked down at her.

"I swear it to you."

"On your honor?"

He looked away and his jaw clenched. Then he turned to face her.

"Yes," he said tersely.

When she remembered to breathe, she nodded, believing him. He was a prince. He wouldn't look her straight in the eye and lie.

"So why me?" she said. "Why be so nice—"

"Call me nice again and you'll regret it." His dark eyes gleamed as he pulled her from the elevator and out onto the street. "I am selfish. I take what I want. Any man would desire you, Grace. In his arms. In his bed. Any man would want you."

"Alan didn't." As soon as the bitter words escaped her, she wished desperately she'd kept them to herself.

"Barrington is a fool." He stopped on the sidewalk. His mouth curved into a sensual smile. "He lost his chance. Now you will be mine. Only mine."

He slowly stroked up the inside of her bare arm beneath her coat, causing her to give an involuntary shudder of longing.

"Grace," he whispered. "Let me show you how truly selfish I can be."

CHAPTER SIX

DECEIT was part of the art of war.

The truth could be a flexible thing in Maksim's opinion. Stretching it correctly was partly how he'd built a vast empire out of nothing. As a teenager, he'd gotten investors by pretending to already have them. He'd deceived competitors, making them believe deals were finished when they weren't. He'd bought commodities cheap and sold them high because he knew information that others didn't. Information he'd ruthlessly kept to himself.

It was not Maksim's responsibility to do the due diligence of others and reveal any truth against his own best interests. He looked out for himself. He assumed others did the same. Only a fool would blindly trust the word of another.

But that was business. Lying in his personal life—that was something new.

And swearing on his honor…

His neck broke out in a sweat to think of it. He'd never looked into a woman's face and lied against his honor. It made him feel…cheap.

I had no choice, he told himself fiercely. *She gave me no choice.* And this wasn't personal. It was business.

Wasn't it?

If he'd told Grace the truth, it would have ended everything. And he was getting so close. He could feel her weakening by the moment.

Seducing her away from Barrington was the best thing that could happen to her, he told himself. The man was obviously using her own feelings against her, working her like a slave without pay.

And it wasn't as if she were an innocent. No, her kisses were too perfect for that. She'd kissed Maksim slowly, sensually, holding herself back with such restraint. As if she'd been born to enflame a man's senses and make him crazed out of his mind with longing until he would do or say anything to possess her.

Even lie against his honor.

He took Grace's hand in his own. "I gave my driver the night off," he said. "I thought we'd walk."

"All right," she whispered, never taking her eyes from him.

Snow whitened the sidewalk, covering patches of slippery ice beneath. He held her arm tightly as they walked past the pubgoers enjoying last call, making sure she didn't slip and wasn't accosted by some drunken lad seeking a beauty for his bed.

Grace was all his.

Maksim could see their breath joined in swirling white puffs of air, illuminated by the moon in the winter night. He looked at her as they walked down the snowy street toward the southern edge of Trafalgar Square.

She looked so beautiful, he thought, lit up like an angel in front of St. Martin-in-the-Fields. Her light blond hair tumbled down her shoulders, looking like spun silver and gold in the frosted moonlight. The diamond tiara sparkled in her hair, making her a spun-sugar princess. No. There was a layer of grief, of steel, beneath the sweetness. She was no helpless pink princess. No. She was a Valkyrie, from a Gothic northern land.

Her shoulders were set squarely, her hands pushed into the pockets of her long black coat that whipped behind her like a regal cape; and yet there was a softer side to her as she leaned up against him, her tender pink lips pressed together, as if she were trying to hold herself back. As if she were trying not to think.

"Thank you for bringing me to your sister's party," she said softly. "I'd forgotten what it was like to be around friends."

He felt another pang of an unpleasant emotion perilously close to guilt. It had been ruthless of him to take her to the party. But he'd wanted to see Dariya on her birthday. And, he admitted quietly to himself, he'd known it would lower Grace's defenses to meet his family. She would think she could trust him. Another lie.

The only thing that wasn't a lie: *he wanted her.*

"Are you, Maksim?"

He focused on her. "Am I what?"

She looked up at him as he led her by Charing Cross station. "Are you my friend?"

He brought her hand to his lips and kissed the back of it. He felt her shiver beneath the brush of his lips against her skin. "No," he said in a low voice. "I'm not your friend, Grace."

They passed down a slender street full of restaurants and pubs, crowds of young people and a few Chelsea football fans in blue-and-white scarves celebrating loudly over a pint. He took her hand and led her down to the embankment by the river. As they walked, they passed a dark garden.

"I don't want your friendship," he said. "I want you in my bed."

The intimacy of his words, as they passed the quiet darkness of the park drenched in crystalline moonlight, was perfect. She looked up at him, her mouth a round *O*. A mouth made for kissing. A mouth he wanted to feel under his.

Right now.

But as he stopped, leaning down to kiss her, she suddenly turned away, her pale cheeks the color of roses in the moonlight.

"Did you learn to flirt like that in Russia?" she whispered. She gave a sharp, awkward laugh and started walking again. "You have some skills."

So his beauty wished to wait? He would be patient. "I grew up here."

Her eyes went wide. "London?"

"And other places." He shrugged. "We moved around. My father couldn't keep a job. We were poor. Then he died."

"I'm sorry," she said quietly. "My father died five years ago, too. Cancer." She swallowed, looked away. "My mother has yet to recover. She almost never leaves the house. That's why…" She looked away.

"Why what?"

She turned back, blinking hard.

"I'm sorry I misjudged you," she said. "Thinking you'd never known what it was like to struggle or suffer just because you're a prince."

"Yes, a prince," he said acidly. "Distantly in line to a throne that, if you haven't noticed, stopped ruling Russia nearly a hundred years ago."

"But still…"

"Prince of nothing and nowhere," he said harshly. "Money is all that matters. Only money."

"Oh, Maksim." Tears filled her eyes as Grace shook her head. "Money isn't the only thing that matters. It's the way you love people. The way you take care of them."

"And you take care of them with money."

"No. Like your sister said, she didn't need more expensive things, she wanted *you*. Your time and—"

"A lovely sentiment," he said sardonically. "But my sister is too young to remember how we nearly starved and froze to death the winter we lived in Philadelphia. After that, I made sure I could support us. I made sure no one and nothing could ever threaten my mother and sister again."

"You protected your family." Her eyes suddenly glittered, and her hands clenched into fists before she stuck them in the pockets of her designer coat. "I should have stayed in California," she said softly. "I never should have left my mother alone."

A hard lump rose in Maksim's throat. "Being with the people you love doesn't always save them. I made my first million when I was twenty, but it couldn't save my mother from dying."

"Oh, no," she said softly. "What happened?"

"Brain aneurysm. She died without warning. I…I couldn't save her."

He stopped, choking on the words. He had never spoken about his mother's death to anyone—not even Dariya, who'd been barely nine when it had happened.

Maksim waited for Grace to expose the weakness in his argument. To point out that, by his own admission, money was indeed not everything in life.

Instead she reached up to stroke his cheek. The first time she'd deliberately touched him.

"It wasn't your fault," she said softly. "You took care of your family. You protected them. You tried to save your mother. You did everything you could."

A tremble went through him, and he involuntarily turned his face into her caress. He closed his eyes briefly, taking a deep breath.

"You're a special woman, Grace Cannon," he said in a low voice. "I've never met your equal."

She gave a short laugh and looked away. The street-lights shone a plaintive blurry light on the dark, swift river beneath the bare trees of the embankment. "I'm not special. I'm completely ordinary."

"You're special."

"It's the clothes."

"It's the woman inside them." He looked down at her. "Grace. You are just like your name. Grace." His eyes narrowed. "And did you say your middle name is Diana?"

"Don't laugh."

"Your mother believed in fairy tales."

"Yes." She shook her head. "But her two favorite princesses didn't live happily ever after, did they?"

"What about you, *solnishka mayo?*" he whispered. His eyes drifted to her lips. "Do you believe in fairy tales?"

She briefly closed her eyes. "I used to believe in them. I used to believe with all my heart."

"And now?"

Their gazes locked, held in the moonlight. Her pupils dilated as she looked down at his lips, then licked her own.

An invitation no man could resist.

Taking her in his arms, he lowered his mouth to hers. Kissing her was heaven. He was intoxicated by the taste of her. The feel of her. His whole body tightened and he drew back to stroke her face, looking down into her eyes. "Tonight," he said hoarsely. "Tonight you must be mine."

He saw her dreamy expression suddenly change to shock. She shook her head hard, as if clearing the cobwebs from her mind.

She hesitated, licking her lips. Then she pulled away from him. "Please. Don't."

He reached for her. "Grace—"

"I can't," she whispered, backing away from his reach. "Please don't."

As she blindly stepped back, he saw her ankle twist, saw one of her shoes slide on the black ice beneath the snow. He heard the snap of one high heel. Saw her stumble back—

He caught her before she could fall. He cradled her against his chest. She looked up at him with an intake of breath. He could feel the rapid beat of her heart. She was so light she seemed to weigh nothing at all. That damned diamond tiara probably weighed more than she did, he thought. And as he looked down into her eyes, he felt dizzy for a reason he couldn't explain. As if he were the one in danger of falling.

A flash of fire burned through him as he felt her tremble in his arms. And he knew that nothing on earth would prevent him from possessing her tonight.

Grace would be his.

Without a word he carried her toward his hotel. As they were about to turn near Savoy Hill, he paused in a nearby alley to lean her against the rough wall and kiss her, hot and demanding. She was all woman, he thought, warm and pliant and willing…but with an elegant hesitation and restraint that heated his blood. He wanted nothing more than to take her against this wall, to fill her up, to slide inside her and thrust deeply until she screamed his name.

"Don't deny me, Grace," he whispered against her skin after he'd kissed her. "Don't deny us what we both want."

The dreamy look had returned to her eyes. "You're right," she said so softly he almost couldn't hear it. "I can't fight you."

She was looking up at him with desire, yes. But also something else. Faith? Trust? Pushing that disquieting thought away, he carried her around the corner toward his hotel. But when he saw the brightly lit porte-cochère of his luxury hotel, he hesitated again in spite of himself.

He wanted her so badly that his whole body hurt from it. But he also had a sour taste in his mouth. Because of guilt? Because he'd lied? He'd lied to get revenge against

Barrington. To win back the merger. To possibly take back Francesca.

But most of all...he'd lied to get Grace in his bed.

She's no innocent virgin, he told himself again. And she wanted him as he wanted her. Maksim had nothing to feel guilty about. Nothing at all.

The doorman saluted respectfully, pretending he didn't see the captive woman in Maksim's arms. "Good evening, Your Highness."

"Good evening," Maksim replied shortly.

He carried Grace straight to the waiting elevator and upstairs to his penthouse. He would make her moan with pleasure, he told himself fiercely. He was so hard with need he couldn't imagine letting her go now.

He couldn't.

Damn it, he wouldn't!

He unlocked his door with one hand then kicked it wide, carrying her over the threshold like a bride. He walked past the stark black-and-white furniture, the black leather sofa, the large flat-screen television above the fireplace.

The curtains had been left open. Below, he could see the dark Thames beneath moving lights of the barges, and steady traffic across the bridges. He saw the gleaming buildings of the city across the river and, to the far left, the brilliantly illuminated dome of St. Paul's.

A fittingly celestial image for the heavenly things Maksim intended to do to Grace. He couldn't even make it to the bedroom before he started kissing her.

In answer, her lips moved against his with gentle hesitation, a light tease that made him plunder her mouth with greater desire. Her kiss was like nothing he'd ever known before. Women had always kissed him so eagerly and desperately, matching his fire or surpassing it. Her unusual restraint fired his blood, increasing his need until he panted from it.

Still kissing her, he set her down on the big white bed. He paused to look down at her. Her blond hair was mussed and tousled. Her eyes were deep pools of blue green, like clear pools of mountain water from newly melted snow.

He trembled as he reached down to touch her, stroking down her neck to the soft silk of her teal dress, down the valley between her breasts to her flat belly. She was so soft and warm. So beautiful from her rose-pink lips to her unpolished nails. He leaned over her, brushing blond tendrils from her face to kiss her cheeks, her neck, her throat. Finally kissing her mouth, he teased her tongue with his as he cupped his hands over her full breasts. Discovering that she wasn't wearing a bra, that those high, firm breasts were unassisted by fabric or padding and were all her, he nearly gasped. He touched her in wonder and felt her nipples pebble and harden beneath his fingers. It was too much for him.

Lowering his head, he suckled her through the silk.

She gave a small hushed cry, arching involuntarily against his mouth. Wanting more, he roughly pulled down the neckline and tasted her flesh. She fell back against the bed with a shudder, exhaling her breath in a little mewling sound that made him harden to painful intensity. Lying on top of her, wrapping his hands possessively around her naked breasts, he suckled her more forcefully, not letting her go even as she twisted beneath him. His body was hard against hers. Feeling her beneath him, he wanted nothing more than to pull up her cocktail dress, unbutton his pants and push all the way inside her with one hard, deep thrust.

The thought made him groan aloud.

He shoved her dress up to her hips, revealing simple white cotton panties. Even that surprised him, compared to the lacy, tarty panties his lovers typically wore to entice him. The simplicity was just like Grace, and revealed the perfection of her curvy hips, her creamy thighs. She didn't need to even try to seduce, to drive any man mad with need…

"Stop," she suddenly whispered. "Please stop."

He realized he'd already pushed up her dress to her waist and had started to unbutton his pants. Damn it to hell, after promising himself he would take his time and make her explode with pleasure, had he really been planning to fill her with one thrust, to roughly and savagely take her body like an animal?

Yes.

What the hell was this sweet insanity? She caused him to lose control. No woman had ever done that before.

"I'm sorry," Maksim said roughly, pulling away. His hands shook with the difficulty of holding himself back. "I didn't mean to go so fast."

"You're not." She licked her swollen, bruised lips. "I'm just…new to this."

He looked at her with a sudden frown. "How new?"

Propping herself up on her elbows, she admitted, "Completely new."

He sucked in his breath.

"Are you trying to tell me you're a *virgin?*"

Her cheeks went red. "Don't say that word!"

"How else would you describe it?"

Tears filled her eyes. "I'd describe it as being helplessly infatuated with a boss who's barely noticed I'm alive, except for one kiss."

"He kissed you?" he demanded. The ferocity of his sudden jealousy surprised Maksim. He'd never felt jealous before, not even when Francesca had delivered her little ultimatum and taken off with another man as promised. But then, Maksim's claim on Francesca had always been territorial. His possession of Grace felt…personal.

Very personal.

She looked at him, surprised. "Why are you so upset?"

Yes, why? "Because…because it's sexual harassment," he stammered furiously. "He's your boss. It's illegal!"

"Sexual harassment?" Grace laughed, then shook her head with a tearful little hiccup. "One drunken kiss before he passed out on the office couch? Then he met Francesca, who I'm sure is perfect at everything. That's why I wanted you to know," she said in a rush. "In case…in case I'm *not* so perfect. I'm sure I'm very clumsy."

Clumsy?

That explained her restraint. Her hesitation. *She was a virgin.* A shudder of hard desire went through him when he thought about how close he'd been to just ripping off her clothes and brutally taking her.

"Maksim, please. The fact that I'm—that word—doesn't mean anything," she pleaded. "It truly doesn't."

Clenching his jaw, he shook his head.

"You're wrong."

She was a virgin. She was doubly innocent.

He couldn't use her in his vicious power play.

He'd been prepared for anything but this. He could fight anything...but this.

Her naive faith had conquered the would-be conqueror.

"Maksim, nothing has changed between us." As she timidly reached for him, he grabbed her wrist.

"No, Grace. No."

He pulled her up from the bed and straightened her clothes. He wrapped her coat around her shoulders. Within two minutes he'd led her down the elevator, through the hotel lobby and out onto the street.

"Where are you taking me?" Grace whispered.

He hailed a passing black cab. When the cab pulled to the curb, he turned to face her.

"You're going home," he said tersely. "Alone."

He pushed her into the cab, then leaned forward to speak to the driver, giving him Grace's address and a very large tip with the fare.

"Wait!" Blinking out of her trance, Grace protested, "No. Maksim, please—"

He slammed the door. "Just go."

"But—"

"Go!" he ordered the cabbie.

The man pressed on the gas. Maksim watched her go. Grace turned around in the back seat to stare at him through the back window. She looked hurt and bewildered.

Then the cab turned a corner, and she was gone.

And for the first time that night, Maksim felt the chill in the air.

Oh my God, he thought suddenly. What had he done? Why had he let her go?

Why had he shown mercy?

He'd always laughed at the word. *Mercy.* Another name for weakness! And he'd let her go. He'd been weak.

He clawed back his hair. He wanted Grace so badly it hurt. Knowing she was an untouched virgin made him ache, wanting her still more. He wanted to take her in his soft, wide bed, to teach her everything he knew, to fill himself inside her again and again and watch her face slowly shine with the joy of discovery. To take her hard. To take her slow. To take her any way he could get her, *and be her first.*

Growling a curse that made the doorman's eyes nearly pop out of his head, Maksim strode into his hotel to his penthouse. He undid his tuxedo tie and tossed it on his desk before he poured himself a short vodka. Every ounce of his body was howling for him to take Grace…take her now…take her hard and deep.

Why had he let her go?

Mercy. Staring down at the swirling clear liquid in his shot glass, Maksim said the word aloud with derision. He gulped the rest of the vodka, but his body still hurt with need for her. He glanced across the room to his vast, empty bed. He could have had her, but he'd let her go.

Tomorrow, he promised himself grimly. Tomorrow he would regain control. He would show no mercy. He would be ruthless.

Virgin or not, Grace would be his.

* * *

The next morning Grace stared forlornly out the small window beside her desk at work.

The snow that had made London so magical had melted, turning to rain. And the rest of last night's magic had melted right along with it.

From their suite of offices on the thirtieth floor, where the Cali-West Energy Corporation had leased space, Grace looked down at the people on the street, far below the other high-rise office buildings of Canary Wharf. The city seemed foggy and sad.

Or maybe that was just her today. Foggy. Sad. With a deep breath, Grace tried to turn her attention back to her computer screen, but her focus on work kept getting interrupted by her painful memories of last night.

She'd sworn she wouldn't surrender to Maksim.

Then she'd not only surrendered, she'd thrown herself at him—and he'd rejected her!

She rubbed her temples, then tried to straighten her wrinkled beige skirt and oversize brown cardigan. She'd planned to iron them this morning but she hadn't had time. She'd tossed and turned all night, then fallen asleep around dawn and had nearly slept through her alarm. Now she felt exhausted. Every time she thought about last night, she writhed inside. Her cheeks burned hot with shame.

She'd tried to resist him.

She'd really thought she could.

But then when he'd shown such unexpected gentleness, allowing himself to be vulnerable in front of her when he spoke of his family, she'd been helpless to fight him.

But she must have overestimated Maksim's desire for

her. Big surprise there. What did she know about men? He'd wanted her—she was still sure about that. Then he'd changed his mind. One moment he'd been kissing her senseless, peeling her clothes off, his hands roaming all over her as he'd pushed her back against his bed.

The next minute he'd been shoving her into a taxi without so much as a good-night.

She swallowed. The reason for the change was obvious. He'd been turned off by her virginity. What man would want to initiate a twenty-five-year-old virgin?

It was all too horrifying.

Sometime before dawn, she'd gotten up from bed and packed up the Leighton dress and coat and the platinum tiara. She would send them to his penthouse tonight and be done.

Even now she could hardly believe that she'd worn them to a society party, where she'd been lavished with kisses by the most devastating man in the city, probably the *world*.

She was lucky he'd rejected her, she told herself. She stared blankly at the screen.

She'd thought she was invulnerable, but she'd utterly lost herself in the winter moonlight. He'd stolen her soul away, evaporating it from her body like mist under his power.

The intoxicating force of his touch had done such strange things to her, made her weak inside, made her melt in his arms. She wondered if she'd ever truly loved Alan at all. Because if she had, how could she have surrendered to Maksim?

As if on cue, she heard Alan's peevish voice. "Where

were you last night? I came back early and you weren't in your apartment."

She looked up to see him standing over her desk. It was almost ten-thirty and he was just now coming into the office. That was typical. What was unusual was that his pale, handsome features looked irritated as he looked down at her.

"I was out," she replied shortly. There was not a single detail about last night that she felt like sharing with Alan.

"Did you finish the wedding plans?"

Anger—usually such a foreign emotion—suddenly burned through her. Did he think she had no life of her own? Did he really think after doing his shopping, she would rush to spend her whole night planning his wedding and honeymoon?

The answer was clear as he waited with his arms folded. *Yes.*

Clenching her hands under her desk, she took a deep breath. It wasn't enough that she came into work before dawn while he never bothered to arrive before ten. It wasn't enough that she'd spent the past three hours frantically writing his speech for a charity event that afternoon, a speech he'd insisted for weeks that he would write himself—until she'd found the task waiting in her inbox that morning.

"Look at these!" The front desk receptionist appeared with an enormous arrangement of exquisite long-stemmed white calla lilies, which she set on Grace's desk. "Aren't they gorgeous?"

"Oh, thank you," Alan said with a smile and a wink,

immediately reaching for the card. "I can't imagine who—"

"Oh no, Mr. Barrington," the receptionist said with a giggle. "They're for Miss Cannon."

"For me?" Grace exclaimed in shock.

"For you?" Alan said with equal shock. "What…who?"

Drawing the card from the envelope, Grace silently read a single line written in a rough, sharp hand.

"Last night you dazzled me like the sun in winter. Waiting outside now for the bright burn of dawn—M."

Happiness soared through Grace.

She hadn't made a fool of herself after all! Maksim hadn't been disgusted with her for being a virgin! He'd just sent her away in the taxi because…

Because he wanted more than just a one-night stand? Because he was trying to protect her and take things slow?

It was the only possible reason.

And he already wanted to see her again! She suddenly felt like tap-dancing beneath her desk.

She closed her eyes and inhaled the heady scent of lilies. Maksim thought she was worth such extravagant beauty.

And for the first time in forever *so did she*.

"Well?" the receptionist asked slyly. "Who's the prince charming, Grace?"

"Yes," Alan demanded. "Who?"

She looked up at her boss and saw him with utterly new eyes. She'd suddenly had enough. Straightening in her chair, she gave a dismissive laugh.

"For heaven's sake, Alan, I'm your secretary, not your wife. Why do you care who sends me flowers?"

"I don't," he stammered, clearly surprised. "I just want to make sure that you devote the proper time and energy to your work."

"You mean the time I've spent buying gifts for your various girlfriends?" she said coolly. "Or do you mean the time I've worked for you around the clock without pay?"

The receptionist gasped a laugh. At Alan's dirty look, she gulped and scurried away.

He looked back at Grace. "Look here, Gracie…"

She leaned her elbows against her desk. "Or maybe you mean the times I've asked you for a pay raise." She thrummed her pen thoughtfully against her cheek. "All the times you put me off and said we'd talk about it later. When I was promoted to your executive assistant. When I moved to London with you."

He swallowed, licking his lips as he attempted a weak smile. "You know how valuable you are to me— how much I need you!"

"I'm afraid that's not good enough."

He leaned over her desk. "Is this because of Francesca? Because you don't need to feel jealous," he whispered urgently. "Our engagement isn't real."

"You bought her lingerie!" she gasped.

He gave a bitter laugh. "I *thought* it was real. She set me straight last night when I suggested an elopement. That's why I asked if you'd started the wedding plans yet—you don't need to bother. She only agreed to a fake engagement to make some other man jealous. She has no interest in marrying me—or sleeping with me either." He clenched his jaw. "But as long as I play along with her, she'll make sure her father doesn't know, and the merger will still go through."

Francesca was trying to make some other man jealous?

Grace suddenly feared she knew who that man might be. And she didn't like it one bit.

"So don't give up on me." Alan gave her his old charming, Hugh Grant smile. "In a few months, it will all be over. Things can go back to how they were. Just be patient. I'm asking you, Grace. Wait for me."

Looking into his smiling eyes, Grace sucked in her breath.

Oh my God.

He'd known.

All this time she'd thought he was clueless about her feelings. But *he'd known about her crush all along.* He'd used her own feelings against her. Used her for free work. Used her for a nice ego boost or a snog when it suited him.

"Well? What do you say?"

"I'm sorry," she said evenly.

And she was. Sorry that she'd given him all her time and energy. Sorry she'd thrown away better opportunities with both hands, while pretending he was the solution to all her problems!

With a sympathetic smile, he leaned against her desk. "Sorry you have to wait?"

"I'm sorry, but things have to change." She slowly rose from her desk. "I'm dating someone else. And if you want me to remain your secretary, it's going to cost you."

He gaped at her. "Where else would you go?"

"I've had another job offer."

"From whom?"

"That's irrelevant," she said. "Since I had to move from Los Angeles, my mother's had trouble paying her mortgage. I need ten thousand dollars to stay working for you. Call it a retroactive raise."

"Ten thousand?" he gasped. "Dollars? Are you joking?"

"And effective immediately," she continued sweetly, "I expect a raise in pay commensurate with the increased cost-of-living expenses in London."

"Grace!"

"So what do you say?" She paused. "Shall I stay and finish writing your speech for the charity event this afternoon? Or shall I clean out my desk?"

He stared at her.

"Stay," he muttered. "Finish the speech. You'll get your raise with your next paycheck."

"And my bonus?"

"Ten thousand dollars? That will take longer."

"You have until Christmas Eve."

He ground his teeth. "Fine. Would you perhaps like to take the rest of the afternoon off, as well?" he suggested acidly.

"Yes, thank you." She smiled at him. "I'll go as soon as I'm done with your lovely speech."

Alan tightened his jaw, then turned away. "Fine."

She almost felt sorry for him as she watched his hunched shoulders as he returned to his office and slammed the door. Almost.

Getting one afternoon off wasn't even close to all the hours she'd worked for free over the past two years, but…Maksim was outside at this very moment, waiting for her. Grace's feet tapped excitedly as she polished the last few paragraphs of the speech, making sure it was perfect before she e-mailed Alan the finished copy. Her spirits were soaring as she put on her old coat and came triumphantly out of the building.

She found Maksim waiting for her at the curb in an ultra-expensive, black Bugatti Veyron.

"Thank God," he said with a dark gleam in his eye as she climbed into the car. "It was agony waiting for you."

"It was twenty minutes."

He put on dark sunglasses. "I'm not a patient man."

She laughed aloud, happier than she'd been for years. "Thanks for the flowers," she said. "They really lifted employee morale. I just got a raise from my boss."

"You lift *my* morale, *solnishka mayo,*" he growled. He reached over to change gears, and his hand accidentally brushed her thigh. "Ready to celebrate?"

"Yes," she breathed.

"So am I," he said, looking down at her steadily in a way that made her feel hot all over. Then he gunned the thousand-horsepower motor, and the Bugatti flew like a black raven through the mist and rain.

CHAPTER SEVEN

GRACE took a deep breath as she stood on the terrace of Maksim's Dartmoor estate, staring out at the snow-dusted fields. They'd left the London rain far behind. Here the moors were wide and haunted beneath the last rays of fading red sun. A thick white mist was blowing in from the sea.

Tears fell unheeded down Grace's cold cheeks. The sound of her mother's happy crying still echoed in her ears as she tucked her cell phone back into her bag.

She'd done it. She'd told her mother that she would save the house from foreclosure. Now Grace would make sure her family never worried about money again. She took another deep breath, grateful beyond words that she'd found her strength. That she'd found herself.

Thanks to Maksim.

Maksim, who'd treated Grace like a princess. She'd never have imagined that any man, let alone someone so handsome and powerful and rich beyond belief, would treat her that way.

Now Grace realized she should accept nothing less. She would never settle again.

She wanted the fairy tale.

She turned from the wide terrace overlooking the carefully tended classical garden and returned through the back door of his eighteenth-century country house. Maksim was waiting.

The inside of the house was every bit as Gothic and misty as the moors outside. Perhaps because the fifty rooms had no furniture—just white translucent curtains that seemed to move against the windows even when they were closed, twisting eerily in an invisible draft that no human skin could feel.

She'd called her mother outside on the terrace, where the cell phone reception was better, and where she could have privacy. She didn't want Maksim to know how desperate she'd been for money. She didn't want him to think of her as someone who needed saving.

She'd been proud to save herself.

She wanted Maksim as her equal. As her friend. As her...lover? She could barely move her lips to form the word, but there it was. Her secret.

She wanted him as her lover.

She wanted him for the fire he sparked inside her. For the way he'd somehow made her become the woman she'd always dreamed she could be. For the dreams suddenly coming true around her, like roses blooming full and red amid the breathless hush of winter.

Grace walked back through the empty salon. Painted cherubs looked down at her from the two-hundred-year-old painting soaring high above the enormous chandelier.

This house was beautiful, large...and lonely.

No one lived here, Maksim had told her. He'd bought

it to use as his weekend escape, but he'd been too busy with work to bother visiting. The caretaker and his elderly wife, who resided in a nearby cottage, were the only ones who'd entered the estate for the last several years.

Until now.

The house seemed happy to finally have company, she thought, then nearly laughed at her own ridiculous thought. The *house* was happy?

What was it about houses that made people so batty?

Grace wiped her eyes as she approached the dining room. She felt like an idiot for crying because she was happy, but as foolish as it sounded, she felt as if her family—as long as they had their home—could survive and be strong.

She entered the dining room, then stopped in shock.

The room was dark, lit by the fire in the marble fireplace—and by dozens of white pillar candles of various sizes and shapes on the floor.

Maksim was lighting the last candle as she entered. He was darkly handsome, wearing a black shirt and black pants. He looked up at her, then straightened as the expression on his handsome face changed to concern.

"You were crying," he demanded.

"Houses," she sniffled, looking with wonder at all the candles. "They don't make a family, except they do, don't they?"

He frowned. "You're not making any sense."

Laughing through her tears, she shook her head. "I'm just happy. I needed money for my house. Thanks to the raise, I'll have it."

"Good," he growled. "About time you moved out of Barrington's basement."

He'd misunderstood her, but she didn't correct him. Moving out of Alan's house *was* a good idea, and as soon as her family's home was secure, that was exactly what she intended to do.

Blowing out the match and tossing it aside, he put his arms around her. "Now leave his office and come work for me."

"Mixing business and pleasure would be a bad idea," she whispered.

He stroked her chin. "I'll buy you a house as your bonus. Any house you want."

She looked around the eighteenth-century country mansion mischievously. "Really? *Any* house?"

He laughed, then he kissed her. His lips were warm and passionate. She felt his rough chin against her skin as his tongue stroked hers, luring her, intoxicating her. She pressed her body against his. When he pulled away, a little sigh escaped her.

"Let me take care of you, Grace," he murmured against her skin.

"I don't want you as my boss," she managed to say. "And I don't want your money. I just want you."

His eyes flickered.

"And I take care of what is mine," he growled.

She was his? The idea of his possession was like a warm blanket wrapped around her. He cared about her. Hadn't he proved that last night when he'd let her go? He could have easily made her a one-night stand, but instead he was wooing her. Courting her in this romantic way.

And she was starting to care about him more than she wanted to admit.

He sat down on a thick white blanket on the floor near the fire. He patted a spot next to him. "Sit down," he said, quirking a seductive eyebrow. When she did, he handed her a flute of champagne.

"Sure, you have champagne," she teased. "But what about furniture?"

Reaching into the hamper, he held out a chocolate-covered strawberry. "I don't need a bed for what I intend to do to you."

She opened her mouth obediently, and he fed it to her. Then she took the next strawberry from the basket and returned the favor. As he suckled the rich chocolate from the lush fruit, he never took his gaze from hers.

She shivered. When she finished the flute of champagne, he took it from her without a word. Gently brushing her hair aside, he kissed her neck. She closed her eyes, shuddering with desire as he nibbled his way down her throat.

"You're so beautiful," he murmured.

And for no good reason, she felt like crying.

"Thank you," she said, opening her eyes to look directly into his. "Thank you, Maksim."

His dark eyes looked surprised. "For what?"

She looked past him, to the translucent white curtains and lead-paned windows overlooking the winter twilight. Shaking with the force of her emotion, she looked into his face.

"It has been a hard few years for my family." She took

a deep breath. "I didn't know what to cling to anymore. Didn't know what to believe in."

Maksim looked at her steadily above the shimmering firelight. His eyes were deep smoke, his strong jawline shadowed with bristle. Surrounded by the flickering white candles on the floor around them, he looked like a dark king from a medieval fantasy.

"Now I do," she said softly, then took a deep breath. "I can believe in you."

He blinked. Hard.

Clenching his jaw, he looked away.

"I'm no saint," he said in a low voice. "I told you from the beginning. I'm selfish. Ruthless."

"You're wonderful." Reaching her hand up to his rough chin, she gently turned his cheek until he looked at her. "I've never met a man like you before. You claim to be selfish and even cruel, but you're not. You're a good man, Maksim. You don't want anyone to know it. You think it's weakness," she said softly. "But I know your secret."

She felt him tremble in her arms. He took a haggard breath, briefly closing his eyes before he looked down at her. His dark gaze shot through her soul. "I've never met anyone like you, Grace. So determined to see the best in people even if they don't deserve it."

"Because of you." She licked her lips with sudden nervousness. "For the first time in my life, I feel brave. Brave enough to…"

Her words dwindled off as the expression in his dark gaze changed, became fired with heat. He stroked her cheek, looking down at her. Their bodies were so close. She could feel every inch of hard muscle, all the strength of his power. Their eyes were interlocked, and in that moment she could hardly say where her soul ended and his began.

"Grace…"

Lowering his mouth to hers, he kissed her. It was a kiss of anguish and longing and such tenderness that a little whimper escaped her.

Then a Russian curse exploded from his lips. He suddenly pushed away from her.

Rising to his feet, he paced in front of her, clawing his hands through his dark hair.

"What is it, Maksim?" she whispered, staring up at him from the blanket. It was the second time he'd pushed away from her. Was something wrong with her? Something about the way she kissed that he didn't like?

Insecurity went through her. She thought of what Alan had told her, that Francesca only agreed to a fake engagement to make some other man jealous.

What if Maksim still loved Francesca?

"It's all right," Grace said miserably. "I understand. I'm not the one you want."

When he spoke, his voice was low. Harsh. "You think I don't want you?"

"It's all right, truly." She shook her head, trying to keep the tears from her eyes. "I'm not remotely your type—"

Falling to his knees, he grabbed her upper arms so tightly that they bruised.

"Not want you? God! Not want you?" he exploded. "All I can think about is taking you, Grace. In the bed, against the wall, on the floor! Not want you? I want to spread your thighs beneath me. I want to caress and suckle and taste you until you explode and shake around me. I want you and every second I physically hold myself back from making love to you is killing me!"

His voice echoed against the soaring ceilings of the empty dining room as it slowly sank in. *He wanted her.*

"Then why do you keep pushing me away?"

He cradled her face in his hands. "Because you are the only sunlight I've known for years," he said in a low voice. "I can't extinguish that warmth in you, Grace. I can't let the world go dark and cold without your light."

"You're afraid to hurt me?"

Clenching his jaw, he nodded.

"Don't be." She took a deep breath. "After my bad experience with Alan, I've decided love is totally overrated." She wouldn't be stupid enough to risk her heart again. No matter how Maksim made her feel. She reached out to stroke his rough cheek, tracing her fingertips down his throat. "I promise you can't hurt me...."

He grabbed her wrist. "Don't," he said harshly.

"Please," she whispered. "Just kiss me."

Their eyes locked.

With a groan, he surrendered.

His lips brushed hers, then bruised her. The rush that spread through her body was unimaginable. He yanked off her coat. He pulled off her oversize brown cardigan. His hands moved urgently over her plain white shirt, undoing the buttons rapidly, pulling the last one until it ripped. He dropped the shirt to the floor and looked at her in the firelight.

"I will try to go slow," he whispered, visibly shaking

as he touched her bare skin. "But the way you affect me, Grace…"

He kissed her again, reaching his strong arms around her, and her white cotton bra fell to the floor. Then suddenly his shirt was off, as well, and pants and skirt all disappeared in a frantic tumble.

And suddenly he was standing before her.

She'd never seen a naked man before. She took a deep breath and looked at him in the firelight. Candles were glowing all around them in the darkness of the empty mansion as she gently reached her hand to stroke him.

He shuddered, jumping beneath her touch.

"You're beautiful," she whispered.

He gasped. Gathering her up in his arms, he laid her gently beneath him on the thick blanket in front of the fire.

She felt the hard muscles of his masculine body, so much bigger and stronger than she would ever be, and as he stroked her naked body in front of the fire she arched beneath his hands. He slowly kissed down her neck, between her breasts, down her belly.

Did he mean to…? He couldn't possibly intend to…?

Moonlight traced the translucent, gauzy curtains. A sudden frozen rain rattled the windows as he pushed her thighs apart.

Lowering himself between her legs, he kissed the inside of her thighs, slowly licking higher and higher. Her cheeks burned and she tried to scoot out of his grasp, but he held her.

Spreading her wide, he tasted her.

Her nipples tightened so painfully that she gasped

aloud. A thousand zinging sensations went up and down her body like lightning shooting out of her fingertips, her toes, her hair. Every nerve was on fire, and she twisted beneath him.

His tongue changed width and pressure, lapping her widely then swirling lightly against her aching nub. She felt dizzy. She was breathless as her body tightened in agony, wanting...wanting...

She cried out as the first burst rolled through her like thunder, starting low and deep inside her and sweeping through her body until she screamed. At that moment he moved his body and pushed himself inside her.

For an instant the pain was wrenching, but pleasure immediately rode behind it, making her shudder in rhythmic contractions around him. As he thrust inside her, she heard his low gasp. With agonizing slowness, he pulled back, then thrust again. She whimpered as increasing pleasure built inside her. Then her hips rose to meet his as he rode her.

He filled her completely. Slowly, steadily, deeper and deeper until he seemed to reach her very heart. The intensity was too much, pleasure so great it was almost pain.

She looked up and saw his hard masculine body over hers, his chest laced with dark hair and his muscles glistening with sweat in the firelight as he thrust inside her. His eyes were closed. She saw the agony on his face as he held himself back, forcing himself to move slowly. His handsome face was taut as he gasped with every slow, deep thrust, filling her to the hilt.

Maksim.

Her prince.

Her lover.

Her…love?

As if he'd heard her thought, he opened his eyes. Their gazes locked, their souls linked. And as he pushed inside her one last time, her world shattered into a million pieces. She shuddered and shook with him so deeply inside her, deeper, deeper, until she felt like she was being ripped in two by his brutally hard body. Her body arched with electricity as she exploded and gasped out his name.

CHAPTER EIGHT

MAKSIM'S intention in bringing her here had been to seduce her. He'd intended to coldheartedly win her loyalty to get information he could use against Barrington. But his conscience had interfered again. He'd tried to resist. To let her go. To push her away.

Until she'd taken him in her soft arms and asked him to kiss her.

In that single instant he'd tossed aside his plans to get information from her. He'd given up his revenge on Barrington. He'd even given up the merger for the sake of possessing her.

He'd given it all up so he could possess her without guilt and be even half the man she believed him to be.

It had taken all his self-control to go slowly. He was determined to make it good for her. But when their eyes met as he slid deeply inside her, when he saw her beautiful face as their bodies joined, he could barely hold himself back from exploding.

He felt her arch and heard her gasp his name; and then he utterly lost control.

Thrusting one last time, he spilled into her with a hoarse, harsh cry that blended with hers. He closed his eyes as his body was racked with waves of pleasure almost too intense to bear.

He collapsed against her. He must have blacked out for a millisecond before he realized he was crushing her with his weight. And he never wanted to hurt her, never, this fragile innocent beauty who'd given him her virginity....

He rolled to one side of her, cradling her softly in his arms, kissing her forehead. She took several deep breaths before she opened her eyes and looked at him. But she did not speak. What had happened between them was too deep for words.

Candlelight and firelight flickered on the lush curves of her naked body. Grace was everything he'd imagined. Just what he'd fantasized about. But she had more than just an innocent beauty—she had an innocent soul.

He was her first.

Maksim gloried in the thought. It filled him with pride and wonder. No other man had ever touched her. No other man had ever thrust inside her—

Then he suddenly stopped breathing.

Distracted by the conflict between his conscience and his overwhelming need for her, he'd forgotten to use a condom. The first and only time he'd ever forgotten.

Turning from her on the blanket, he stared blankly at the high ceiling. Barely visible cherubs smiled down at him from the shadowed depths.

What if there were a child?

"Maksim." Grace rolled her naked body over his. He

felt the soft press of her breasts into his chest as she looked down at him with concern. "Did I do something wrong?"

"No." Wrapping his arms around her, he kissed her on the temple. "Don't think that, *solnishka mayo*. Never think that."

She ducked her head, placing her cheek against his heart. "Do you feel like you've betrayed Francesca?"

Francesca? He was trying not to think about her— something astonishingly easy to do, considering she'd been his mistress for a full year. He set his jaw. "Why ask me about her? Do you feel you've betrayed Barrington?"

She shook her head. "I never loved him. That was infatuation, nothing more."

For reasons he couldn't explain, those words seeped into him, relaxing him like a warm embrace. He stroked her naked back lazily, appreciating the curve of her body and sweet, smooth skin. "I'm glad to hear that. So there's nothing to stop you from coming to work for me."

"But I thought you said I shouldn't endure sexual harassment from my boss?" she teased.

"You'll enjoy it from me," he growled.

"A lovely offer." She sighed, then slowly shook her head. "But I can't desert Alan. I feel sorry for him."

"Why? He's gotten the deal—and the bride."

"But he just found out she never intended to actually marry him. They haven't even slept together. She's just trying to make some other man jealous." She took a deep breath, then lifted her eyes to his. "I think it must be you."

His hand stroking her back stilled.

"It's not a real engagement?"

"The merger is real. Her father doesn't know. But the

engagement will end." She licked her lips. "And you can have Francesca back, if you want her."

For a moment Maksim couldn't even breathe.

He couldn't believe it.

What a joke of fate. The moment he'd decided to surrender to his conscience, the moment he'd decided he wouldn't try to force information out of Grace— she'd tossed the key to destroying Alan Barrington right into his lap.

With this one bit of information, he could destroy the merger.

Part of him had suspected this all along. Francesca had been so furious when Maksim hadn't caved to her ultimatum in October. After a tempestuous year together, a year of screaming breakups and passionate makeups, she'd demanded that he marry her. "Or else," she'd threatened ominously, "you'll lose me." But Maksim never responded very well to threats or ultimatums. In reply he'd kissed her until she sagged in his arms, then he'd whispered, "In that case, I must lose you."

Typical of Francesca to orchestrate her battle by going straight to his enemy. Managing to string Barrington along without even giving him her body— Maksim was impressed. But the fact that she'd never intended to actually go through with her threat to marry him revealed her weakness.

All Maksim had to do was tell the Earl of Hainesworth the truth, and the merger would be his. Along with Francesca, if he wanted her....

"Do you love her, Maksim?" he heard Grace whisper. "Do you?"

He abruptly focused on the sweet, beautiful girl in his arms.

Grace was so different from his former mistress in every way. She was curvaceous, with full cheeks the color of roses, skin that glowed with health, and natural blond hair that looked like blended gold and silver in the candlelight.

Francesca was tiny and thin in ultrachic designer clothes, with fiery red hair that came compliments of an expensive salon. Natural? Francesca was the type of woman who wore red lipstick to bed!

Grace was poor, young and sweet, and so kind-hearted that she let others take advantage of her, while Francesca gleefully bossed the servants and rode all over anyone weaker than herself.

Grace was honest to a fault. Even now, Maksim could see the vulnerability in her eyes as she anxiously looked at him. Francesca savored nothing more than a viciously well-placed lie. She planned her love affairs like a chess match, or possibly like a general leading troops into a war she intended to win.

"She's so beautiful," Grace said, biting her lip. "She's the kind of woman any man would want."

It would be easy to hurt Grace, Maksim thought. And he never wanted to do it.

"I'm with you now." He rose from the blanket and swiftly blew out the candles around them before he nestled back against her, pressing his naked body against hers. He cuddled her in his arms, turning them both on their sides toward the fire.

With a little sigh she relaxed in his arms. In no time

at all he felt the even rise and fall of her breath as she slept peacefully against his chest. Trustingly.

Normally after he'd been with a woman, he couldn't leave her fast enough. But with Grace, he felt different. She made him feel strangely at peace.

He stared at the fire, waving and crackling and dying in the marble fireplace.

He could complete the merger. Get his revenge on Barrington. Get everything he'd dreamed of: he could create and control the largest oil and gas company in the world.

Or…he could do the unimaginable.

He could forget he'd ever heard the information. And keep Grace as his mistress.

He'd planned to spend the winter in Moscow after the merger was done. He could bring Grace to live in his new Rublyovka estate. He rather liked the idea of having her cook for him, bustling about, making him laugh, sharing his bed at night. How better to keep himself warm through the long, cruel Russian winter?

He could open her credit accounts at all the luxury shops in one of the most expensive cities in the world. He could hire a tutor to give her Russian lessons.

And Maksim could give her other kinds of lessons as well. Personally. He suspected the recent virgin would be a quick and eager student….

Her only job would be to be his mistress, enjoy his company and spend his money. She would be happy.

Maksim stared at the hypnotic dwindling of the fire. Could he let Barrington win? Could he let the merger go? Could he give up his dream of world domination—

and let Barrington have it, while he slipped into a distant second place, possibly making his own company ripe for an eventual hostile takeover?

Giving up this merger meant potentially losing everything he'd ever fought for. But the choice before him was plain.

Grace or the merger.

He couldn't fool himself into thinking he could have both. If Grace found out he'd betrayed her, using her careless words in bed against her boss, she would never forgive him.

But if he didn't betray her, would he ever be able to forgive himself?

Maksim held her in his arms as the moonlight flooded through the high windows. The dying firelight flickered in the sleek marble fireplace.

He'd never appreciated this house quite so much before. Never appreciated anything quite so sharply as this moment. He knew it would never come again. She sighed in sleep, her breasts swaying beneath his arms. He felt himself stir. This woman moved him like no other.

Her eyelids fluttered. She looked up at him with dream-drenched eyes.

"I think I love you," she whispered.

His body went absolutely hard. So hard it hurt.

She blinked. "Oh my God, did I say that aloud? I thought I was dreaming."

"You said it out loud," he said tersely.

"I just meant—"

"I know what you meant."

He gripped her.

She'd just experienced sex for the first time, he told himself. That was what she meant. She loved him in the way a man loved a well-cut suit or a perfect steak or watching sports on Sunday; or crushing an opponent to win a big business deal. She loved him in the way a person loves a pleasure they never want to end.

He told himself these things, but he knew they were lies.

"Maksim…" She touched his shoulder.

"Go to sleep," he told her harshly.

The fire had turned to ashes before he heard her finally fall back into slumber. But he couldn't sleep. He lay awake all night, watching as the pink dawn rose over the misty-white moor.

He had to make a choice.

The warm light of dawn sifted through the high windows, revealing the dust motes trembling in the air. He woke her with a kiss. On her shoulder. On her temple. All over her naked body.

She turned over with a sigh, blinking and not quite awake, but she held out her arms for him. Instinctively welcoming him into her soft body. Into her soft heart.

But this time, as he tenderly made love to her in the pink fresh light of dawn, he used a condom.

Horrible. Unbearable.

When could she leave?

Grace glanced at the clock on her computer screen and tapped her toes impatiently on the floor. She didn't want to be at work on Christmas Eve!

Apparently, no one else wanted to be here, either, since she was the only one left in the office. She'd come to tie up a few loose ends before her two-week vacation in Los Angeles. She smiled as she thought of home. She just needed to wait long enough to pick up the check for $10,000 that would save her mother's house.

But Alan was, of course, late.

Grace was trying to focus on compiling the necessary data for Cali-West's fourth-quarter sales reports. But her mind kept wandering to her favorite subject.

Maksim.

The past two weeks had been the most wonderful of Grace's life. Maksim had taken her out nearly every day. He'd taken her dancing. Out to dinner. And it was hilarious how he kept trying to buy her things. Like yesterday, when he'd suddenly pulled her into a car dealership in South Kensington and wanted to buy her a gold Maserati convertible.

"To match your hair," he'd said, then smiled. "Think of it as a hair accessory."

When she'd refused, he'd tried to argue with her. "It's a small Christmas present," he'd said. "A trifle. A token. *A stocking stuffer!*"

He'd really made her laugh with that one.

She'd steadfastly refused, of course. But later that night in his penthouse suite, he'd made her an offer she could not refuse—he'd made love to her all night.

That must be why she felt so tired today. So absolutely exhausted, and even a little bit queasy.

Especially when she thought about leaving Maksim for the next two weeks.

She was falling in love with him.

She'd already fallen like a brick!

So much for her defenses. Thank God he wasn't in love with Francesca as she'd briefly feared, because she'd started to fall in love with him from the moment he'd taken her virginity in that empty house on the snow-swept moor. She'd even stupidly blurted it out.

Fortunately, by some miracle, telling him she loved him just days into their relationship hadn't scared him off!

Perhaps he was starting to care for her, as well.

The thought made her heart leap in her chest. She wanted to buy him a Christmas present before she left, but what did you get a man who truly had everything? Her naked body wrapped in a big red bow?

Grace glanced down at her form-fitting gray cardigan, yellow silk blouse, pearls and gray wool slacks. Her clothes weren't quite so glamorous as the Leighton cocktail dress, but they were fresh and pretty and new. She grinned down at her feet. She even had new shoes, lovely pale-pink pumps of such sturdy quality that they would never break. They squeezed her a little in the toe, but who cared about that? They were beautiful. She'd put her first paycheck since her raise to good use.

She wanted to look nice for Maksim.

A stronger wave of queasiness went over her. Grace glanced at her lukewarm coffee cup, feeling ill. Had she drunk too much wine last night at dinner with Maksim? Impossible, she remembered, she'd had just half a glass. It must have been the chicken tikka, then.

Picturing the spicy dish, usually her favorite, she felt so nauseated that she almost retched over her keyboard. Rising to her feet, she stumbled to the ladies' bathroom just in time.

Afterward, as she came out of the bathroom she still felt a bit sick and in a cold sweat. She was just grateful she was alone in the office.

Then she saw she wasn't. Alan stood by her desk.

Oh, thank heaven! He was here with the check, and that meant she could go! Hang the data for the fourth-quarter reports. No one would compile the information until January, so why kill herself over it? She'd collect her bonus, brush her teeth then go to the penthouse to see about convincing Maksim to come home to California with her for Christmas.

If all else failed, she'd convince him via that big red bow. She giggled. Perfect.

But she still felt a bit dizzy as she walked toward her boss. "I'm glad to see you!"

"Are you, Grace?" Leaning against her desk, Alan's pale eyelashes blinked rapidly as he stared down at her. He looked strangely grim.

Something seemed to be bothering him, but Grace still felt queasy and couldn't dredge up enough energy to wonder what it was. "Alan, if you'll just give me my bonus check, I think I'll head out. You don't mind if the sales figures wait? I'm not feeling very well." When he folded his arms and continued to glower at her, she added weakly, "It *is* Christmas Eve…"

"You can take as much time as you want."

"Oh, thank you—"

"Because you're fired."

She stared at him for a long moment. "What?"

"You heard me. You have exactly three minutes to pack up your desk before I have you thrown out."

"Is this a joke?"

"Yes, a joke. The secretary I trusted most just betrayed my secrets and caused me to lose the deal of my life."

"What?" she gasped. "How?" She frantically tried to remember saying anything to anyone. Had she mentioned any details? The numbers, the price? She shook her head. "I never breathed a word to anyone!"

"Lord Hainesworth just pulled his funding and support," he said furiously. "He found out this morning the engagement was fake. I've lost the deal and now I'll likely lose my position as CEO. The board has been after me for the past year. I've lost everything. My only consolation is...*so have you.*"

Oh my God, what had happened?

"It's got to be some ghastly mistake," she said. "I would never betray you. Please, I need that bonus—"

"Bonus?" He barked a laugh. "You're lucky I don't have you thrown in jail for corporate espionage! You'll never get hired again by anyone if I can help it. No job recommendation. No back pay." His lip curled. "Now get the hell out before I call the police."

"But I didn't tell anyone about the fake engagement," she cried. An icy trickle went down her back. "Except..."

"When you blackmailed me into giving you a raise, you didn't mention that you were already working on your back for Maksim Rostov!"

She sucked in her breath.

"It wasn't like that," she gasped. "How did you find out about—"

"Francesca heard it from her friends." Alan shook his head with a derisive snort. "Apparently he's been flashing you all over town, his cheap little mistress. You've always been so desperate for money, Grace. Tell me. What did you enjoy more—selling him my secrets or selling him your body?"

She felt like he'd just slapped her across the face.

"I didn't sell anything," she whispered. "He wouldn't do that to me."

"No? You think Rostov wanted you for your intelligence?" he sneered. "For your beauty?" He looked her up and down. "You might have gotten new clothes, but you're way out of your league. This was always a game between him and Francesca—always. He dumped her. She wanted him back. And now they're together."

"No!"

"If you really believe he would choose you over her, you're even more stupid than I thought." He turned his back on her. "I'm sending the security guard up here in two minutes."

Numbly Grace gathered up a few items from her desk, putting a half-dead plant and two framed pictures of her family into a box. She left the building, then realized she'd forgotten her old coat. The security guard refused to let her back inside. Her only option would be to call Alan and ask him to bring it down to her.

Instead she left without it.

Outside, there was a biting chill in the gray afternoon sky. Clutching the cardboard box to her chest, she shivered in her thin cardigan and silk blouse.

Alan had to be wrong. Maksim wouldn't have betrayed her!

She pictured his darkly handsome face. The way he'd

teasingly fed her chow mein noodles at his penthouse last week. The way he'd tried to trick her into accepting expensive gifts. He'd made love to her. He'd made her laugh. He'd been her first.

He wouldn't use her careless words in bed against her, the words she'd spoken when she'd been feeling insecure and had been seeking reassurance!

But she hadn't told anyone else about the fake engagement. Who else could it be?

The answer was shockingly clear.

He'd intended all along to seduce and betray her.

No. A sob escaped her. She felt dizzy as she walked toward the nearest Tube entrance. Another wave of nausea went over her and her knees shook as she went down the escalator. As she sat on the half-empty train, she felt the curious and pitying stares of other passengers. She knew what they saw—a woman without a coat, red-eyed and holding a box with a plant and picture frames. Easy to follow that story. Sacked on Christmas Eve.

Just sacked—or also betrayed?

She found all her clothes stuffed in two suitcases sitting outside her basement flat in Knightsbridge. The locks had been changed. Alan had tossed her out.

Pulling her cell phone from her handbag, she dialed Maksim's number.

No answer. After three rings, it clicked over to voice mail, to his terse voice saying, "Rostov. Leave a message."

Another wave of dizziness washed over her. She started to leave a message. "Maksim, I've just heard something that can't possibly be…"

Her phone went dead. She stared down at it in shock. It had been her business phone, paid for by her company. Alan must have had it disconnected.

Grace took a deep breath, trying to control the rising panic.

She placed her family photos in the suitcases, wrapped herself in her warmest, thickest, frumpiest sweater and left the box and plant in a nearby rubbish bin. She managed to get back on the Tube, dragging both suitcases behind her.

Could it be true?

She heard the echo of his voice. Husky. Deep. Slightly foreign. *I have been accused of having no heart. I am telling you the truth, Grace. Take this as a warning.*

Struggling with her luggage, she came out of the Tube stop near his hotel. He was likely not there but busy at his office, as he hadn't answered his phone. She would wait for him in the penthouse and...

Then she saw he wasn't busy in the office.

Maksim was walking arm-in-arm with Francesca.

He looked ruthlessly handsome in a gray suit and coat. The redhead at his side wore an ivory coat and six-inch heels. Grace watched in shock as they passed the smiling doorman and went inside his hotel.

She saw the look Francesca gave him over the shoulder. Flirtatious. Cozy. Affectionate.

And Grace felt her knees go weak beneath her.

Trembling, she stumbled out into the road to flag down a cab. She shoved the suitcases inside and collapsed in the back of the black cab. "Heathrow," she gasped to the cabbie.

She could no longer deny the painful truth. She'd loved him, while he…

He'd taken her virginity to win back another woman.

Grace needed to get home. Her mother would take her in her arms and stroke her hair and tell her everything would be all right. Her mother knew about broken hearts.

Grace nearly cried with gratitude when a desk clerk at the airport managed to switch her seat to an earlier flight.

Crossing the Atlantic that endless day, crammed into a middle seat between two large, snoring men who both hogged the armrests and overlapped her space, Grace kept her eyes tightly closed. If she started crying, she was afraid she wouldn't be able to stop.

She had more to worry about than a broken heart.

How would Grace save the house? How would she support her family? Now that her father's life insurance was gone, her family was nearly destitute. And the economy was tough. How would Grace find employment when she'd just been fired for blurting out a billion-dollar secret in bed?

Grace clutched the thin airplane blanket to her chest. Funny to think she'd been so determined to not accept any gifts from Maksim. She'd returned the tiara and Leighton clothes. She'd refused his offer of the Maserati convertible and a new house and his many other suggestions of jewelry and clothes and luxury trips. She'd been so proud to stand on her own two feet. So proud to show Maksim she wanted *him,* not his money.

But money, it seemed, was all Maksim had ever wanted. Money. Revenge. Another billion or so dollars to pile on top of his fortune. She'd given him her virginity and her heart, but he'd only wanted money.

Money...*and Francesca.*

CHAPTER NINE

"SHE'S not here."

Maksim looked up to see Alan Barrington staring down at him from the doorway of his town house. It was dark and gray, past twilight on Christmas Eve.

He'd been knocking on the door of Grace's basement flat for the past five minutes without answer. He hadn't expected to be so late. He'd promised he would take her to the airport for her late-night flight, but secretly he'd planned to talk her out of going home for Christmas. His private jet was waiting at a small nearby airport to whisk them away to the South of France.

But he was fifteen minutes late. Only fifteen minutes—that was something of a miracle, given all the surprises today! The merger was nearly a done deal. Thanks to Francesca, it had fallen into his lap, and he'd have been a fool to refuse. But he'd left the meeting halfway through. His people could mop up the details.

He wanted Grace.

He'd called her as soon as he got out of the meeting but hadn't been able to reach her. "Where is she?"

Barrington glared at him. "Why would I tell you?"

"Her phone was disconnected. Any idea why?"

The man folded his arms. "The phone went with her job, which she lost this afternoon."

"After all her loyalty, you fired her so quickly?"

"Loyalty? Some loyalty. Isn't it enough you already took one woman from me? Now you want the other one?" Barrington turned his lips into a sneer. "I'm not her pimp."

In three leaping steps Maksim had run up the stairs and grabbed him by the throat. "Are you calling Grace a whore?"

"Let me go!" the slender man croaked.

Maksim released him with a growl. "Apologize."

"Oh, so now you're her protector?" The blond man gasped, rubbing his neck. "You did this. You seduced and betrayed her. Not me."

"I never betrayed her," Maksim said, even as that strange, unpleasant prickle snaked down his spine. Guilt?

"Why bother denying it now?" Barrington snarled. "You've won. You've taken the merger. You've taken Francesca. You've gotten your payback—you've gotten rid of me for good. My shareholders have already issued a statement asking for my resignation."

"Good." But at this moment, Maksim's revenge didn't feel very satisfying.

"What do you care about some secretary?" Barrington looked at him with shrewd, beady eyes. "You have Francesca."

Right. Francesca.

Maksim's capricious ex-lover had shown up at his penthouse that morning, offering him Barrington's head on a silver platter. "I've just told my father the truth," she'd said, weeping artful tears from her lovely green eyes. "I never wanted Alan. It was you, Maksim, always you!"

Maksim's furious retort had been interrupted by the ringing of his cell phone. Francesca's father had moved swiftly. He'd always preferred that his company accept the offer from Rostov Oil; only his daughter's fake engagement had made him consider Cali-West. Within half a day the merger proceedings had been well started, although it would take another several weeks before they would be fully signed, sealed and delivered.

Maksim had accepted the deal. But he'd chosen Grace. He'd never used the information she'd shared. He'd never betrayed her.

But he realized now it'd worked out exactly the same as if he had.

He clenched his fists. "Just tell me where she is."

"Flying to Los Angeles, I expect, with the plane ticket I bought her. I hope it crashes." Barrington slammed the door.

Coming down the steps from the Knightsbridge town house, Maksim dialed his private investigator to get her address. But that wasn't all he discovered about her family's situation.

An hour later he was on his private jet en route to California.

The little yellow cottage gleamed in the predawn darkness, a shining beacon on the cliff above the soft roar of the Pacific Ocean.

Breathing heavily after her uphill walk, Grace crept back into her house, tiptoeing as she walked past the artificial Christmas tree decorated with ornaments from her childhood, gleaming with colored lights.

"Gracie?" Her mother suddenly peeked around the kitchen door. "You're awake early. I expected you to sleep in this morning."

Grace hid the small purchase she'd bought at the twenty-four-hour drugstore half a mile away. "Um. Jet lag. I couldn't sleep, so I went on a walk."

"Oh, poor dear," her mother said sympathetically, then brightened. "I'll make you some coffee. Come chat while I baste the ham."

"I'll be right there, Mom." Grace tried to calm her rapidly beating heart as she went to her childhood bedroom. She changed out of her jeans and back into her soft, comforting flannel pajamas and red chenille robe.

She set the bag down on her nightstand.

Her mother had been so happy to pick her up at L.A. airport last night, so joyful that she'd come home even earlier than expected. The boys had jumped up and down as they got her luggage from the carousel, and even seventeen-year-old Josh had hugged her, saying in a low voice, "I'm so glad you're home."

Her mother had driven them in the minivan back home to the northern beach town of Oxnard, an hour away, then made them all hot chocolate at midnight with marshmallows. Everyone finally went to bed to dream happy Christmas dreams.

Except Grace.

She hadn't been able to tell them that they were about

to lose the house they were sleeping in. She'd lied. No, not lied, she told herself angrily. Lying was for selfish bastards like Maksim. All she had done was put off the truth that would break their hearts. But she'd barely been able to stomach the hot chocolate, which was usually her favorite. A low-grade nausea had been with her for two days. As she went to bed late that night in her old bedroom still decorated with posters of rock bands and old teddy bears, even her breasts hurt.

That's when the dreadful thought first occurred to her. Nausea…dizziness…exhaustion. Painful breasts.

And so she'd sneaked off before dawn to buy a pregnancy test.

It's a waste of money, she told herself firmly. She and Maksim had only had sex a few times—all right, *many* times—but only just that once without protection. Fate wouldn't be so cruel, would it?

She'd been too carried away, too overwhelmed by sensation to even think of using protection that first time. If she'd thought about it, she would have assumed that a playboy like Maksim would naturally make sure he didn't get his many lovers pregnant. Especially lovers he intended to betray.

Her heart still hurt to think about it.

But the pregnancy test would have to wait. She couldn't take it now, knowing her mother was awake and waiting for her.

Grace went slowly into the kitchen. Sitting at the dining table, she could barely tolerate the smell of the creamy, sweet coffee her mother happily served her. But that was nothing compared to being forced to listen to her mother's delighted praise as she tearfully thanked Grace for saving their family.

"I was silly to live in denial and hide from our problems. You've inspired me with your career, Gracie. I've run this home for twenty years," Carol Cannon said as she put homemade biscuits in the oven. "After raising you four children, I can do anything!" She paused thoughtfully. "I might go back to school to become a tax accountant. I was always good at math."

Grace gulped down a single sip of hot coffee, scalding her tongue. The coffee made her feel nauseous, so she put it down immediately. "I know you can do anything you want, Mom."

Her mother's eyes glistened at her. She leaned forward to kiss the top of Grace's head. "I'm so proud of you, Gracie. I want to come with you tomorrow when you take the check to the bank. I'm so grateful to have such a strong daughter to lean on."

Grace rubbed her temples, feeling like a fraud.

They had no savings. No income now that she'd lost her job. In just one week, they would have to leave their beloved seaside cottage and beg their friends and family for a place to stay. And as there were five of them, including three boisterous teenage boys, they would soon wear out their welcome with even their most devoted friends.

I'll tell Mom tomorrow, Grace promised herself over the lump in her throat. *I just want her to enjoy Christmas.*

The rest of the morning was agony for Grace, as she watched her younger brothers open their presents and saw their joy and the grateful hugs they gave their mother. The gifts would all have to be returned to the store tomorrow. They would need every penny to survive. Seventeen-year-old Josh would have to say farewell to his long-desired iPod. Fourteen-year-old Ethan would be forced to give back his new guitar. And twelve-year-old Connor would tearfully have to return his new drums. Even their mother would return the expensive cashmere sweater the boys had bought for her with their own money earned mowing the lawns of neighbors throughout the fall. When Grace opened her own present from her family, she found a large hardcover picture book about the Trans-Siberian Railroad. Looking up at their beaming faces, she felt like crying.

"Thank you," she said over the lump in her throat. "I love you so much."

"It's 'cause you're such a world traveler," her youngest brother said happily. "I helped pick it out."

At brunch Grace watched her mother serve the platter of ham and scalloped potatoes. The boys cheered the food, but all she could think was that the ham alone was worth two weeks of cheap dinners like ramen noodles and frozen bean burritos.

Tomorrow, she repeated to herself, pasting a frozen smile on her face. *I'll tell them tomorrow.*

But after brunch, when her mother and brothers got ready to attend a Christmas-morning service of songs and carols, Grace pleaded jet lag and stayed home.

Now, finally alone, she stared at the pregnancy test, waiting for the results.

Be negative, she willed with every creative visualization technique she'd ever heard about on morning talk shows. *Be negative.*

Her hands shook as she waited for the results. She squinted in the dark bathroom. Would there be one line? Or two? She thought she saw the lines start to form. She couldn't see.

She ran out into the front room with the sunny windows overlooking the sea. The prewar cottage was small and bright and cozy, with old striped couches and cushions they'd had since Grace's childhood.

She looked down at the test. Negative. It would be negative....

Two lines. Oh my God. Two lines. Positive.

She was pregnant!

She heard a sound and turned to look.

Maksim stood in the open doorway. Brilliant sunlight cast him in silhouette, leaving his features dark. His wide, powerful frame filled the door, instantly filling their cliffside cottage with the force of his presence.

For a moment she thought her knees were going to buckle beneath her. In spite of everything, her heart soared to see him. She longed for him to take her in his arms and tell her everything Alan had said was a lie. To tell her he'd never seduced her to get information about the merger and win back a woman a thousand times more desirable than Grace could ever be.

Thrusting the pregnancy test in her robe pocket, she took a deep breath.

"What are you doing here?"

He stepped over the threshold, his eyes focused only on her. "I came for you."

A shiver spread through her body. She could barely

breathe as she faced him. She gripped her old chenille robe more tightly around her body. "You shouldn't have come."

He strode forward, his face tense. "You shouldn't have left London."

She lifted her chin.

"Why?" she said coldly. "Are there other secrets I might have forgotten to blurt out to you in bed?"

His handsome face closed down, looked grim. "I never betrayed you."

"You didn't take the deal with Exemplary Oil?"

He clenched his jaw. "I took it yesterday."

She briefly closed her eyes. So Alan hadn't lied. Everything he'd said was true.

"You must love her very much," Grace said, her voice barely a whisper.

He shook his head. "Grace, listen to me…."

She sucked in her breath, hating him more than she'd ever hated anyone in her whole life. "What are you even doing here? Shouldn't you be celebrating with Francesca?"

"No, damn you!" His steel-gray eyes blazed as he grabbed her by the shoulders. "I don't want her. I want you!"

"On the side?" She gave a harsh, ugly laugh. "You really think you can have anything you want, don't you? You always intended to seduce me for information, from the moment your car splashed me in the street!"

The rage in his eyes faded. His grip on her shoulders loosened.

"You're right," he said in a low voice. "You were nothing more to me then but Barrington's secretary, and

I thought you were his mistress. I intended to use you to take back what was rightfully mine."

"You took my virginity for that." She fought the angry tears rising to her eyes. She would die before she'd let him see her cry! "What is wrong with you? Don't you have a soul?"

His jaw clenched. "When I made love to you, I gave up my plan," he said, looking down at her. "I couldn't use the information you'd told me in bed. I knew I would lose you. So I kept silent. Francesca was the one who told her father. It would have been foolish and useless for me to refuse the deal she brought to me yesterday." He lifted her chin, holding her in his arms. "But I swear to you. On my honor. I never betrayed you."

She wanted to believe him.

Wanted it so badly it hurt.

But she couldn't.

"You mean the same word of honor," she said evenly, "with which you swore you weren't trying to use me against Alan?"

"My only lie," he ground out. He looked at her, and his eyes glittered. "I hated lying to you. But I made the choice, Grace. I chose you."

He stroked her cheek, looking down at her with emotion. She closed her eyes, her heart pounding at his touch.

"Come with me to Moscow," he whispered. "I want you with me. As my secretary, as my mistress, whatever you—"

Her eyes flew open. "Your...secretary?"

She ripped away from him. After everything they'd

been through together—the romance that had consumed her so utterly that she'd fallen in love with him and was about to have his child—that was still how he saw her. As a secretary?

And now that he'd won the merger with Exemplary Oil, he wasn't even trying to hide it. He was no longer even vaguely trying to pretend that he cared for her.

"You mean because I've helped you steal a billion-dollar deal from my last boss," she said scornfully, "you'll kindly allow me to type your letters and make your coffee in Moscow? Except you'll want different fringe benefits than Alan, I suppose. I assume I'm to spend my evenings and weekends earning my wages on my back?"

His dark brows lowered furiously as he grabbed her shoulders. "You know that's not how it is—"

"You want to hide me away in Moscow, so you can enjoy Francesca in London!" The images she'd seen of Francesca with him outside the hotel went through her. "Marrying her is part of your deal, right?"

"Damn you!" he shouted. "I don't want her! I want—"

"I saw you with her yesterday!" she shouted back.

He dropped his hands from her shoulders. "What?"

Tears filled her eyes. She wiped them fiercely. "After I was fired, I went to your hotel. Stupid me, I actually had faith in all the lies you'd told me."

"They weren't lies, not all of them—"

"Oh, yes, I always get things wrong, don't I?" She could barely speak over the lump in her throat. "Because I'm just a silly little secretary. That's all I've ever been to you."

"You little fool," he ground out. "You know that's not true—"

"Stop trying to have it both ways!" she shouted. "You never cared for me, you just took my virginity, you seduced me, you got me—" *Pregnant with your child,* she almost blurted out, but she stopped herself just in time. Humiliation gnawed at her, causing her cheeks to go hot.

She didn't want to tell him about the baby. Ever.

She just wanted him out of their lives for good.

"I did you a favor to get you away from Barrington," he ground out. "You were letting him walk all over you!"

He'd felt sorry for her?

"Oh, thank you. Thank you so much," she said. Waves of acute misery continued to build inside her, making her feel more ill by the minute. "I wish to God I'd never let you touch me!"

Gut-wrenching nausea waved over her. Covering her mouth, she ran to the bathroom, stumbling on the floor to retch over the toilet just in time.

She heard him come in behind her. His voice was suddenly gentle as he said, "But Grace, you're ill."

"It's nothing—the flu—just go!" She wiped her mouth, looking back at him with eyes of fury. "I hate you!"

"Grace—"

"Just go! You liar, you back-stabbing bastard!" She grabbed a bar of soap and threw it at him. He ducked it easily, enraging her still more.

"I'm not leaving you."

"If I'm sick," she bit out, "it's because looking at your face makes me want to puke! My skin crawls when I think of how I let you touch me." She looked at him with eyes of ice. "You're not a prince—you're not even a *man*."

She'd finally pushed him too far.

He stiffened behind her.

"Fine." His lip curled. "Now that I know your true opinion of me, I won't fight to keep you. I see now there is nothing for me here…"

Turning to go, he stopped.

Bending over the carpet, he picked up something that had fallen to the floor and rolled across the carpet.

The pregnancy test had fallen from the hole in her pocket!

She gasped, rising quickly to her feet. "It's not what you think. It's nothing…an old test…a friend's…left here," she stammered helplessly.

"You're pregnant." He looked at her. "You're pregnant?"

She stared at him. She wanted to deny it, but the lie stuck in her throat.

"Am I the father?"

She gasped at the insult.

"You know you are! Although I wish to God you weren't. I wish any other man on earth was the father but you!"

His eyes focused on her coldly. "And I realize now everything I ever thought about you was wrong. I thought you were special. You're not. You're selfish and deceitful. Jealous and controlling."

She gave a harsh laugh. "More than your precious Francesca?"

"Francesca and I broke up because she tried to push

me into marrying her. You did something far worse. You were going to let me walk right out that door, weren't you? You were going to keep my child a secret. You intended to sacrifice our child's need for a father, and live in poverty without even a home, all for the sake of your own selfish pride!"

He knew the house was in foreclosure? She gasped, feeling as if he'd exposed her vulnerable jugular.

"How did you know?" she whispered.

"I told you. I protect what is mine. That means my child. That means his family." His lip curled. "And whether I wish it or not, that means my child's mother." His eyes were cold as he looked down at her. "You will be my wife."

His...wife?

She sucked in her breath.

His duty bride, the ignored spouse he would leave trapped in a lonely Muscovite palace while he continued to pursue the wickedly lovely Francesca in London?

"No," she whispered desperately. She looked around the sunlit cottage. She desperately wanted her family to keep their home. Then she thought of the tiny life in her womb who needed to be protected. Better to remain in poverty in the warm sunshine of California, near family who loved her, than risk either of them anywhere near Maksim's icy Siberia of a heart!

She shook her head hard. "How many times do I have to say it? I don't want your money!"

"But now you will take it." His voice was low, dangerous. His gray eyes glittered at her as he added maliciously, "As you will take my name. Today."

"No! I won't!"

He grabbed her painfully by the shoulders. "Apparently, I haven't made myself clear. You have no choice."

She was suddenly afraid of him, this dangerous man who seemed to control his anger with such icy reserve.

"Your wife in name only?" she whispered.

He gave a hard laugh. "And now you think to trick your way out of my bed? No. You will be my wife in every way. You will sleep naked in my bed and service me at my will."

It was the final stab to her heart. He'd already made it plain he cared nothing for her. He expected her to surrender her body to his possession, without affection, without love?

"You're worse than Alan," she whispered. "A million times worse. Because, you're not asking me to be your wife. You're trying to make me your household slave, chained to your bed."

He stroked her chin.

"I'm not asking you," he said coolly. "I'm telling you. You are pregnant with my child. You will be my wife. Every jewel and home and luxury you could possibly desire will be yours. You are now mine."

He was offering her money, in exchange for giving her body and soul to a man she hated—a man in love with another woman! "A gilded cage. You're offering me the life of a whore!"

He grabbed her wrist, pulling her hard against his muscular body.

"Have it your way, then. You will be my pretty songbird in a golden cage." He kissed her cruelly, punishing her. As she felt her lips bruise beneath his embrace, a whimper escaped her. He drew away with a hard smile, looking down at her with a gaze like frozen steel. "And, my beautiful one, you will sing only for me."

CHAPTER TEN

MOSCOW, ancient stronghold of czars, was white and frozen in the breathless hush of winter. The sprawling modern city of untold wealth was as brutal as Maksim's will, Grace thought. And in the frosty twilight of New Year's Eve, it was as cold as her husband's icy heart.

Grace stared out the window of her large, elegant, lonely bedroom. After nearly a week in this vast city of old poverty and new wealth, her only outings had been to the doctor and to the exclusive shops of Barvikha Village and Tverskaya Street, driven by bodyguards in a Humvee with darkened windows. She'd shopped beside powerful oligarchs and their pouting trophy girlfriends dripping with furs and diamonds.

She'd seen little of the city. She'd seen traffic, traffic and more traffic on the paved, guarded road to Rublyovka. She'd seen huge billboards on Moscow's ring roads, advertising luxury cars and jewels as they drove past old buildings with aging Communist icons chiseled in stone.

For a woman who'd once hated fancy shops, they were now her only excuse to escape her luxury compound. Surrounded by bodyguards and servants, Grace was never alone.

And yet she was always alone.

She was a captive bride in a guarded palace, and she'd been forced to accept she was completely in Maksim's power. He'd made that clear by coldly marrying her in Las Vegas on Christmas Day.

Once her family came back from their Christmas service, Grace had been forced to tell her mother she was pregnant. Then she lied and said she loved her baby's father. She'd endured her family's delighted surprise and her mother's whispered blessing on their hasty elopement. When she learned they had no ring, Carol had wrenched off the precious ring that hadn't left her finger for twenty-seven years.

"Your father would want you to have this," she'd said to Grace, holding out the simple half-carat diamond ring in rose gold as tears streamed down her face. "He would be so happy for you today. I just wish he could be here now."

Grace had blinked back her own tears two hours later, as she gave her vows to Maksim in the small chapel of the Hermitage Resort, a Russian-style casino owned by his friend, Greek tycoon Nikos Stavrakis. And Grace hadn't been blinking back tears of joy, either. Beneath the candlelight and mournful, painted Russian icons, she'd pledged herself to Maksim for life. Barely looking at her, Maksim had tersely done the same.

After their cold wedding, there had been no sunny honeymoon. Maksim had brought her to Moscow on his private jet and abandoned her in his luxurious palace compound in an exclusive neighborhood outside the city. Grace had no idea where he'd spent his days and nights since they'd arrived. She tried to tell herself she didn't care.

Her only consolation was that her family was safe. They would never lose their home or be worried about money again. Maksim had paid off the entire mortgage and had placed a large sum in a bank account to make sure her family would always be financially secure and her brothers could go to college. They were happy because they believed Grace was, too.

She had been well and truly bought.

I'm sorry I did this to you, baby, she thought, rubbing her flat tummy mournfully. She looked around the large, feminine bedroom with the blue canopy bed and the lady's study beside it. Down the hall, the next room was empty. Maksim had ordered her to create the baby's nursery there, but Grace didn't have the heart. She couldn't accept her new life here. Couldn't accept that this was all the home life her child would have.

As purplish twilight fell softly over the skyline of the distant city, Grace finally saw his armored car pull past their front gate.

Where had he been for the past six days? Where was he sleeping at night? Clenching her hands into fists, she rose from her chair at the window and left her bedroom.

From the high second-story landing overlooking the wide marble floors of the downstairs foyer, she saw Maksim enter the house, followed by assistants and bodyguards. His face was dark and tired. He didn't bother to ask the housekeeper about how his new bride was faring. He didn't bother to even glance upstairs. He simply handed Elena his coat, went into his study and closed the door behind him.

For Grace, it was the final straw.

She ran downstairs. Without knocking, she pushed through his study door.

Sitting at his desk, he looked up at her with infuriating calmness. "Yes?"

She hated his coldness. She envied that he had ice water in his veins instead of blood. She wished she, too, could feel nothing, instead of feeling like her heart was continually breaking anew!

"Where have you been?"

He barely glanced at her as he gathered papers on his desk. "You have missed me, my bride?" he said sardonically.

"I'm your wife. I have a right to know if you've been sleeping with someone else!"

"Of course you do," he said with a cold laugh. "I can tell you I've been working day and night to finish details on the Exemplary merger, sleeping two hours a night on a cot in my office. But of course you will immediately know I have been with another woman. You will immediately suspect I've set up Francesca in a suite at the Ritz-Carlton."

Grace's heart fell to the floor.

"Francesca's in Moscow?" she whispered.

His lips twisted into an ironic smile. "And to think I once believed you had such faith in people."

"You destroyed that!"

"Have no fear, my dear wife," he drawled. "I have no interest in Francesca. How could I, when I have such a warm, loving wife waiting in my bed at home?"

His barb went straight to the heart. She clenched her hands into fists. "Just try getting into bed with me sometime, and you'll see how warm and loving I am!"

Maksim rose wearily from his desk. "Enough." Placing a stack of papers in his briefcase beside his laptop, he started walking toward the study door. "If you have nothing else to discuss, I'll wish you good-night."

She stared at him incredulously. "You're leaving? Just like that?"

He stopped and turned back to her. At the intensity of his expression, she trembled from within.

Then he lowered his head and kissed her softly on the cheek. "*Snovem godem,* Grace," he said softly. "Happy New Year."

She turned her face up toward his, her heart aching with the memory of the man she'd loved in London. She searched his gaze for some remnant of the man she'd laughed with, cared for. *Loved.*

Then he turned from her.

"Don't wait up."

Anguish rose in her heart…then anger. She hated his coldness. How could she have ever thought he was a good man?

"You can't keep me locked up here!"

He glanced back curiously. "Do you not think so?"

"I'm not your slave!"

"No." He gave her a brief, cool smile. "You are my wife. You are carrying my child. You will live in comfort and luxury, with nothing to do but enjoy the pleasure of your own company."

"I'm going insane!"

"How surprising."

She ground her teeth in frustration. "It's New Year's Eve. Elena is going to Red Square…"

Her voice trailed off as she saw him shaking his head.

"There will be half a million people in Red Square. The bodyguards couldn't protect you."

"Protect me? From what?"

He shrugged. "I have enemies. Some hate me for my billions, some hate me for my title. You could be kidnapped for ransom. It's rare but it does sometimes happen. Or perhaps—" he glanced at her keenly "—you'd be tempted to run off in the crowd."

"I won't," she said tearfully. "Please. I just want to live a normal life!"

"Just what every princess wants," he said sardonically. "And cannot have."

He turned away.

"Maksim, please don't leave me here," she whispered. "I can't bear to be left like this."

He paused at the door, not bothering to turn around.

"Have a pleasant evening, my bride."

She stood in shock in his office until she heard the front door slam and the silence as his bodyguards and assistants left with him.

She walked slowly up the wide, sweeping stairs to her lonely bedroom.

He'd left her alone on New Year's Eve.

Was it really possible that Lady Francesca Danvers was in Moscow?

Very possible. The fiery, tempestuous redhead was the woman Maksim had really wanted all along. The woman every man wanted.

She tried to tell herself she didn't care. But still, her heart felt perilously close to despair.

"Can I bring you something to eat, princess?" Elena said softly, and Grace looked up to see the older Russian woman standing in the doorway. She liked the capable housekeeper, who supervised a staff of twenty and spoke fluent English.

But between nausea and fury, food was the last thing on Grace's mind. She shook her head.

"You must eat something, Prince Maksim said, for the baby."

"He's not the boss of me!" Grace shouted, then she felt instantly abashed about her childish behavior when she saw the expression on the housekeeper's face. "I'm sorry, Elena." She paced the luxurious room, then rubbed her forehead. "I'm going out of my mind. I've been trapped in this house for days."

"I'm sorry you're not feeling well, princess. I'm sure His Highness was very regretful to have to leave you alone. He's very busy."

Grace closed her eyes as grief and fury built inside her. Yeah. She could just imagine how he was *busy*.

All week she'd been waiting…for what? For him to

return to the man he'd been in London, the man she'd loved? For him to act like a decent, caring husband?

Well, she wasn't going to wait anymore. She wasn't going to remain jailed here for his convenience!

Grace went to her huge closet and grabbed dark skinny jeans and a snug black cashmere sweater she'd bought at the Leighton boutique on Tverskaya Street. "I'm coming to Red Square with you tonight."

Elena looked alarmed. "Have you asked Vladimir and Igor if it's all right?"

There was no way Grace was going to invite her hulking, overprotective bodyguards to join her tonight! "No. I'll just take the Metro with you."

"It's the train. And, princess, I'd get fired for sure."

"Please, Elena!" She closed her eyes. "I just want a nice, normal life. Just a few hours to breathe fresh air and blend in without big bodyguards hovering over me wherever I go!"

"You don't know this city. You don't speak a word of Russian."

"I do know one word. *Nyet*. And that's my answer to Maksim." She pulled her hair into a ponytail. "*This* princess will have a normal life. I might be his wife, but I won't be his slave!"

Grabbing her warmest coat and hat, she opened the second-story window, peering down at the wide wall. She'd have to climb over on the tree branch and down the other side...

"*Kharasho,*" Elena said, sounding resigned. "You can come with me. Just stay close and don't wander off!"

Grace nearly wept tears of gratitude. "I promise I won't tell Maksim!"

"He will find out," the woman said with a shake of her head, then grumbled, "For a new bride to be home alone on New Year's Eve? Bah!" And she muttered something under her breath in Russian.

Grace tapped her black boots on the floor. Every muscle in her body ached to get out of this luxurious palace. Away from her captivity and loneliness.

Away from the fact that she was with yet another man who was in love with Lady Francesca Danvers instead of her.

Was it Grace's fate to always lose every man she cared about to the same woman?

The painfully ironic thought chased her all the way to Red Square an hour later. They followed the currents and crush of people past the twin towers of the Resurrection Gate, with its mosaic icons of favored saints, into Red Square.

"Stay close," Elena said.

Grace took one look at the colorful onion domes of St. Basil's Cathedral and gasped. Standing still in the packed crowd, she slowly turned around, looked at the Kremlin, Lenin's tomb and the red buildings around the square. She'd dreamed about this ever since the Soviet breakup when she was a girl.

Red Square was lit with a million lights and filled with half a million cheering people. It was more fantastically beautiful than she'd ever dreamed. For one moment it made her forget her pain.

Then she saw a nearby man take his girlfriend in his

arms and kiss her. Watching them kiss and laugh and share an intimate moment just a few feet away suddenly made Grace ache twice as much with loneliness.

She turned back to Elena, but the Russian woman was gone! Somehow they'd been separated.

Struggling not to feel alarmed, clenching her gloved hands into fists and shoving them into her coat, Grace looked around through the white mist of her breath.

She felt so alone, and the night was so cold. Here in the far north of the world, she wondered if winter would ever end.

Suddenly she felt a hand on her shoulder.

She turned and saw Maksim standing beside her!

In spite of everything, her heart leaped to see him, dark as night in his black clothes.

"You little fool," he ground out. "I expressly told you not to come here."

She took a deep breath. "I'm not your prisoner."

He looked down at her grimly. "If you risk my child without bodyguards again, you will be."

The threat made her furious. How dare he insinuate that she'd placed their unborn child at risk, just by living a normal life?

"I'm sick of you trying to control me." Furious, she tossed her head, "And where's Francesca?" she taunted. "Don't tell me you've finished with her already?"

"Damn your jealousy," he growled.

"I'm not jealous," she fired back. "I don't care if you make love to her every night. I don't love you. I don't want you!"

He yanked her into his arms.

"Who's lying now?" he growled.

Her eyes suddenly widened when she saw his intent. "No—"

Lowering his mouth on hers, he kissed her savagely.

Beneath the colorful fireworks in the dark wintry sky, he punished her in his embrace, plundering her lips, mastering her with his strength. She tried to resist, pushing at his chest with her small hands, but in the end her own desire overpowered her in a way brute force could not. Surrendering, she sagged in his arms with a whimper, holding his body against hers as she returned his brutal kiss with equal passion.

Beneath the brilliantly lit onion domes of St. Basil's Cathedral, they kissed in a fiery embrace of hate and longing amid the roar of half a million people celebrating the birth of the new year.

From the day he'd married Grace, Maksim had intended to punish her.

And he'd done it. He'd brought her to Moscow, a place where she knew no one, and he'd deserted her in the same palace he'd once dreamed of bringing her to live as his mistress. Except all the tenderness he'd once had for her was long gone. In its place was cold, hard anger.

He'd rushed to her in California. He'd told her the truth. He'd practically begged her to forgive the single lie he'd told her. A small request considering that he'd been willing to give up what he wanted most for her sake.

He'd treated her with better care than he'd ever treated any woman. *He'd placed her interests above his own.*

And all he'd gotten from her in return were insults—and lies. Then, to top it off, she'd tried to steal his child!

He'd thought Grace was different. That she was special. But he knew the truth now. She might have been a virgin when he first bedded her, but in other ways she might as well be Francesca—selfish, cruel and controlling.

When Elena had told him Grace had accompanied her to Red Square against his orders, he'd been furious. Then he'd been frightened—purely for the baby's sake, he'd told himself.

But when he dismissed Elena and saw Grace looking so forlorn and alone amid the festive crowds of Red Square, anger and desire and fury had finally boiled over him.

And something more. Desire. The desire he'd suppressed for days, trying to finish the hellish, endless details of the merger. The desire he'd tried not to feel, staying away from the bride he despised as a way to keep himself from wanting her.

He hadn't meant to kiss her. He'd sworn to himself when he brought her to Moscow that he wouldn't even touch her.

Then she'd taunted him.

Anger and lust had seized him. And he'd seized her. Now…

His need to punish her blended with his need to possess her. Taking her by the hand, he dragged her from the crowds of Red Square to his waiting car. Closing the privacy screen to block the eyes of his bodyguard and driver, he threw her into the back seat and kissed her hard. Her hat had been long lost. Pulling off her coat and gloves, he pressed her body beneath his, kissing her with angry force. She returned his kiss with matching fervor, biting at his lips until they bled.

"I hate you," she breathed against his skin.

For answer, he ripped her black sweater off her body. Yanking her bra to the floor of the car, he pressed his mouth on her breasts, biting and suckling until the mix of pain and pleasure made her gasp and arch beneath him.

"Hate me if you want. You are mine to do with as I please," he said, licking her nipples. "You will pleasure me."

"I won't...ah," she sucked in her breath as he moved his hand between her legs, over her tight jeans, rubbing her until she gripped his shoulders wordlessly seeking release.

He wanted to rip off her jeans. He wanted to thrust inside her hard and deep, until she begged for mercy.

Until she begged his forgiveness.

By the time they made it home, her lips were bruised with his kisses, her blond hair tousled and tangled, her eyes dazed and bewildered with her unwilling longing. Giving his driver and bodyguard a terse order in Russian, he collected Grace in his arms and carried her roughly into the house.

The palace was quiet. The bodyguards were outside celebrating in the guardhouse by the gate. The rest of the servants had been given the night off.

Maksim intended to carry her to the master bedroom, but halfway up the stairs she reached up to stroke his neck and he could bear it no longer. He placed her down on the curving, sinuous staircase, beside the art deco railing that looked like swirls of melting wax in white limestone. Pulling off her jeans, he undid his fly. He was hard as a rock and aching for her.

He didn't tease her.

He didn't ask permission.

Without warning, without tenderness, he pulled down his pants and thrust himself inside her, all the way to the hilt.

She gasped, then moved beneath him, her full, heavy breasts swaying as she arched her back, pulling him deeper still.

She wanted him as unwillingly as he wanted her. He knew it. But suddenly he wanted far more than just to take his pleasure. He wanted her to take her own. To force her to hold nothing back. To surrender herself completely.

Rolling over, with his own back against the shallow, wide steps, he lifted her on top of him. She gasped as he lowered her over him, impaling her.

"Move," he ordered.

As he commanded, she slowly moved against him, sliding her wet, hot body against his in circles that got progressively tighter and smaller. He felt her muscles clench around him, deep inside her, as she closed her eyes. She stopped, fighting her desperate desire.

He stroked her breasts, then, taking one of her hands in his own, he sucked gently on a fingertip. Her blue eyes met his, innocent, shocked. Her pupils were dilated, her nipples painfully tight, her body so hot and wet around him. And as if she could not resist his will, she started to move again. Her heavy breasts bounced softly as she rode him, pushing her hips harder and faster until he was barely able to hold on to his self-control. He looked up at her beautiful face, at her soft, curvaceous, feminine body that was getting tighter and tighter around him as she started to shudder. And he heard a low scream rising from her throat.

As she moved herself against him, rocking back and forth in rhythm, her core slick and impossibly soft around him, he felt her start to tense and shake, and finally he could take it no longer. With a Russian curse on his lips, he exploded into her with a shout that echoed against the high walls of the foyer, mingling with her own ecstatic cry.

Exhausted, her limp body fell against his own. For a moment he held her, feeling her soft body against his chest, listening to the sound of her breath.

But when his sense returned, he was furious.

At her.

At himself.

He had no self-control whatsoever where Grace was concerned.

He'd sworn to himself that he wouldn't touch her. But this proved his desire was stronger than his pride. Proved she still had control over him.

Proved that no matter what she thought of him, he still cared for her.

Pushing away roughly, he rose to his feet on the stairs, furious at himself. Without saying a word, he rezipped his pants and coldly left her on the stairs.

The palace suddenly felt too confining, and outside

he would be watched by guards. With a deep breath, he climbed two floors to the roof garden. Where he went to find peace. Where he went to be alone.

The rooftop terrace was covered with snow and dead branches of the dormant garden. He took several deep breaths, stretching his arms, trying to clear his head. He stared at his own breath, looking past the treetops and lights of the city toward the distant fireworks in the cold clear night.

He heard her come out though the garden door. He couldn't believe she'd followed him out here. He looked at her with narrowed eyes. She'd put her clothes back on, tying her tattered blouse together as best she could. She hesitated, then finally came up behind him, wrapping her arms around him.

For a moment he was tempted to lean into her arms. His heart hungered for her.

Then she spoke.

"Just tell me the truth, Maksim," she whispered. "Admit that you betrayed me. Admit that you lied and I'll forgive you."

His jaw clenched as he turned to face her. "You'll forgive me," he said tersely.

She swallowed, then lifted her chin. "I will try."

Anger rushed through him, pulling away all his remembered tenderness like an overflowing river ripping sediment from the banks.

"I do not want your forgiveness," he said in a low voice.

"Maksim." Her face was tear stained, her voice a whisper. "Just tell me if you love her. Tell me."

Love her? *Her?* Who?

Then he knew. Of course. She was talking about Francesca. He'd never given Grace any reason to feel jealous, but she continued to grind away at him with her insecurity's endless need for control.

Did he need further proof she thought him a man without honor, a man she couldn't trust?

He'd tried to change her mind in California. He wouldn't try again. He wouldn't allow himself to be vulnerable with her. Never again.

He looked at her coldly. "In two days I will introduce you to all of Moscow as my bride. You must be ready for the ballroom reception. You and the child need rest. Go sleep. In your peaceful, solitary bed."

"Maksim…" she whispered.

For answer, he turned and left her without a backward glance, leaving her shivering and alone on the snowy rooftop garden, in the chill black night beneath icy white stars.

CHAPTER ELEVEN

"LADY Francesca Danvers is here to see you, princess."

Grace whirled around in her chair. "What does she want?"

"Nothing good, I wager," Elena said sourly.

Grace turned back to face herself in the mirror. She hardly recognized herself. Wearing a long, sparkling, champagne-colored gown that caressed her body, with her blond hair piled high on her head, she looked like a princess.

For the past two hours, Elena had been helping her get ready for the ballroom reception that would introduce her to Moscow society. But she wasn't sure she could face the woman her husband still loved. She licked her lips nervously. "Do you know her?"

The Russian housekeeper shrugged as one of the maids brought in a small enamel-and-silver box. "She was here once before, long ago. But old lovers should disappear when a man gets married," she said with a sniff. "Let me send her away. Your reception starts in ten minutes. You don't have time to speak to each and every guest before…"

"She's a guest?" Grace gasped. "Who would have—"

But she cut herself off. She didn't have to ask who would have invited Francesca.

She closed her eyes, willing herself not to cry. It would ruin the carefully applied makeup, and she had to look lovely when she was introduced as Maksim's bride.

He must really hate her, to do this, she thought. How could he stab her in the heart, forcing her to publicly meet his mistress? It hurt so badly she thought her heart might crack in two.

Maksim had made his feelings plain. After they'd made love on New Year's Eve, she'd begged him to justify his actions. She'd been so desperate for a fresh start, she'd offered him almost more than she thought she could bear—her forgiveness. If only he would just admit what he'd done, and promise never to see Francesca again!

But he had refused. And in the two days since, he'd avoided her more than ever.

And yet she still couldn't believe Francesca was in Moscow.

When Maksim had said he'd installed her in some fancy hotel, Grace had assumed he was just trying to hurt her.

But the woman was here. Had he been telling her the truth? Had he been spending all his nights with his mistress?

Why shouldn't he? She thought miserably. He'd only married Grace because she was pregnant. A forced marriage wouldn't necessarily stop him from loving Francesca....

"Ah, you look perfect. You just need one last thing.

His Highness sent this." Elena pulled an antique gold-and-emerald tiara from the enamel box and reverently placed it around Grace's high chignon.

"It's beautiful," Grace said in a low voice.

"It used to belong to the prince's great-aunt, the Grand Duchess Olga." Elena pulled back to see the effect in the mirror then nodded her approval. "Now I'll send that wretched woman away," she added, "and I'll be right back."

"No," Grace blurted out, her mouth suddenly dry. "Send her up."

The Russian woman looked at her dubiously. "Are you sure, princess?"

No. "Yes."

A moment later Lady Francesca was escorted into the drawing room beside Grace's bedroom.

The pale redhead was as beautiful as Grace remembered. Petite and very thin, she wore a pink tweed Chanel skirt suit and white peep-toe shoes with flashy red soles. In her perfectly manicured hands, she carried a white quilted bag with a gold chain handle.

She glanced around the pretty, elegant, feminine room. "I see you've set yourself up nicely," she said with a sniff.

"Please sit down," Grace said nervously, indicating the blue high-backed chair. "May I order some tea?"

"No, thank you." Francesca's cold, kohl-lined green eyes looked right through her scornfully. "This isn't a friendly visit." She set her handbag on the tea table, all business. "I've come to ask you how much money I have to pay you to divorce your husband."

Grace stared at her in shock, speechless.

"Oh, come on," she said impatiently. "You were clever enough to get pregnant. You are hoping to profit from your child. I don't blame you. I'm sure I would do the same if I had no money, skills or beauty. So just tell me how much you expect."

Grace tried to speak, but still couldn't.

Francesca pulled her checkbook and an expensive-looking pen out of her wallet, then looked up at her. "Well?"

"I'm not trying to profit from my child!"

"Because you're a decent mother?" Francesca's red lips twisted. "Can we please skip your fervent protestations? We both know that Maksim should belong to me. Tell me how much it will cost to be rid of you."

Remembering all that she'd suffered because of this woman, Grace clenched her hands into fists.

"I gave up one man to you without a fight," she said in a low voice. "I won't do it again."

"So you did have a desperate little crush on Alan," Francesca drawled, glancing down at her flawless scarlet nails. "I wondered. My dear, don't you realize that a woman like you cannot possibly compete against a woman like me?"

Every word was like a stab to Grace's heart. "I never loved Alan," she said in a trembling voice. "You can have him. But I'll die before I give Maksim up to you!"

"You poor fool. I understand Maksim in a way you never will." Francesca tilted her head. "He doesn't love you. If you were any sort of decent woman, you would let him go. If you won't, you're not a decent woman.

You're a gold digger who deliberately got pregnant to trick Maksim into marriage."

Grace's insides twisted. "I never tried to get pregnant. I never asked him to marry me," she whispered. "He insisted."

Francesca nodded. "So you didn't want to marry him in the first place. Perfect. Then take my check and leave him. Find some other man to marry." She stared at Grace with false sympathy. "Someone more at your level."

"He's my husband and father of my child. Now we're married, I won't give him up." She narrowed her eyes, looking up at the other woman as her shoulders shook with emotion. "Not to you or anyone."

With a sigh, the beautiful redhead closed her checkbook. "Fine. Have it your way." She leaned forward across the tea table. "You're not a bad person. I can see that. So if you love him, let him go."

Grace looked up at her rival. "You love him?"

Francesca's green eyes were clear and direct. "And I can help him. In life. In business. I thought a fake engagement would prod him into setting a date to marry me. But he plays the game even better than I do. He actually married you." She gave a thin red smile. "I told my father about the fake engagement to save Maksim's merger. I can make him the richest man in the world. What can you ever do for him…except be a burden?"

"Izvenitche, pojhowsta." Elena suddenly appeared in the door, scowling. "It's time for the princess to make her entrance at the reception."

Francesca rose gracefully to her feet. She paused at

the door, her eyes narrowed and her red lips pulled back to reveal her sharp white teeth.

"If you love him, Miss Cannon," she said softly, "you'll leave him."

After her parting shot the beautiful redhead swept away, leaving pain and regret racking through Grace in waves.

Maksim had told her the truth. Francesca was the one who'd told her father about the fake engagement. Maksim had tried to tell her he didn't betray her. He'd seduced her, yes, but he hadn't been able to use her words against her. He'd protected her honor at the expense of his own. He'd given up what he wanted most—for her.

But she hadn't believed him.

Instead she'd insulted him. She still winced to remember the horrible words she'd thrown at him when he'd followed her to California.

She'd done everything she could to push him back into Francesca's arms. Could he ever forgive her lack of faith?

He has to, she thought. *Even if I have to beg him for forgiveness.*

But what difference would begging make—if he was in love with another woman? She closed her eyes as a stabbing pain went through her heart. Why would he ever choose her over Francesca, after the way she'd treated him?

"Are you ready, Grace?"

She turned to see Maksim standing in the doorway. She sucked in her breath. He looked devastatingly handsome in his tuxedo, her dark Rostov prince, strong and powerful and very, very dangerous.

"She's ready," Elena said approvingly. She adjusted

the tiara over Grace's high chignon, adding pins to hold it as she said softly, "And the most beautiful princess the house of Rostov has ever seen."

Maksim slowly looked her over and then nodded. "You are beautiful."

Grace's heart fluttered in her chest. "You are, too. So handsome, I mean."

His dark eyes were inscrutable as he held out his arm. "Come."

He led her out of the room to the top of the elaborate limestone staircase where they'd made love with such intensity two days before. At the bottom of the stairs, she heard the noise and voices of their guests, the clinking of crystal. She couldn't face them as Maksim's wife.

Not without knowing their marriage had a chance.

She stopped in her tracks, pulling on his hand with urgency to pull him back into the hallway.

He looked down at her impatiently. "What is it?"

"I should have believed you all along. I'm so sorry, Maksim." Her eyes filled with tears as the words spilled out, rushing over each other. "You never betrayed me. Francesca said she told her father about the engagement. Oh, Maksim. Can you ever forgive me?"

His eyes narrowed. "You have spoken with Francesca?"

"She was here."

His eyebrows rose. "Here? What was she—"

She placed her hand over his. "I don't want to fight," she pleaded. "I want to start fresh. To go back to how we were in London. I believe you now. I'm sorry I didn't have faith—"

"It's easy to believe me now, isn't it?" he interrupted

coldly. "You believe Francesca's words, when you wouldn't believe mine."

This was all going wrong. She'd apologized, begged him to forgive her, pleaded for a fresh start. What else was left? What hadn't she said?

Only one thing, and it terrified her. She couldn't possibly lay her soul bare before him, not when his face was so cold, his body so tense and unyielding.

"Come." He turned away, drawing her once more toward the wide sweeping stairs and the marble-floored foyer where she knew hundreds of society guests were waiting.

She grabbed his tuxedo sleeve, pulling him to her, forcing him to listen.

"Maksim, I…" Her heart pounded in her throat. She licked her lips. "I…I love you."

His steel-gray eyes widened, became deep pools of some emotion she couldn't identify, but it caused yearning and fear to spread through her veins.

"I love you," she repeated, her mouth utterly dry. "And I have to know. Can you ever love me?"

She waited for his answer, and as the seconds ticked by, they seemed to last for eons.

Then his handsome face slowly turned to ice. He shook his head grimly. "It's too late."

"How can it be too late?" she gasped.

"I'll always take care of the child, Grace." He looked away, tightening his shoulders. "But I'll never love you again."

Again?

He'd loved her?

He'd loved her—and she'd thrown his love away!

"No!" she cried. "It can't be too late! I love you. And if you once loved me…"

He gave her a sardonic smile, all emotion gone from his eyes. "And how well you repaid me."

"I made a horrible mistake." She was humiliated by the whimper in her voice, but she couldn't lose him. Not now. Not when she'd finally realized he was truly the man she'd always wanted. "Please, Maksim…"

"Stop begging," he said harshly. "You are a princess. Begging is beneath you."

"I can't lose you." She felt a sharp pain in her heart. "But I already have, haven't I?" she whispered. "You want to be with her."

"Who?"

"Do I have to say her name?"

His jaw clenched as he exhaled with a flare of his nostrils. "I am sick of having to defend my actions where Francesca is concerned. You are my wife. You are pregnant with my child. There will be no other woman in my life. There can't be. How clear do I have to make it?"

"But if there were no baby?" she said, her heart in her throat. "Would you still have married me?"

"That is a pointless question. There is a baby. The decision has been made. Love doesn't matter."

She closed her eyes to block out the pain. "You're wrong," she whispered. "It's all that matters."

Maksim had married Grace out of honor. The honor she'd bitingly, insultingly accused him of never having. And for the sake of honor, he was determined to stand by her side.

But if Grace hadn't been pregnant, he would have gone to Francesca like a shot. His heart was with her. She was beautiful and wealthy and a perfect match for Maksim in every way.

"I will always protect you both," he said in a low voice. "Don't ask for more than I can give."

He would protect her with money and his name. Nothing more.

Grace's own parents had had such a blissful marriage. She thought of how they'd laughed together, teased each other. The way her father had playfully wrapped his arms around her mother's waist while she cooked in the kitchen. Her parents' love had shone through everything, especially their children. Grace and her brothers had shared such a happy childhood beneath the umbrella of their parents' love.

She suddenly realized it had never been their house that had made them a family. The house hadn't made them secure and warm. It had been her parents' love. Their mutual adoration that had endured long after her father had died.

The lump in her throat sharpened.

What kind of home life would Grace's loveless marriage create for their baby?

How would their son or daughter feel, raised by a father who'd been forced to give up his own happiness because of the child's very existence?

Grace suddenly felt like crying.

Maksim held out his arm stiffly. "Come. Our guests are waiting."

Her heart felt shattered in her chest as he escorted her down the limestone Art Deco stairs.

In the wide marble foyer, beneath the soaring crystal chandelier, she saw a swirl of faces. Hundreds of people applauded for her as she was introduced as Her Highness Princess Grace Rostova. Gorgeous women in diamonds and Maksim's billionaire friends cheered in both English and Russian, holding up their champagne flutes in a toast to the new princess.

Grace got a glimpse of herself in the enormous gilded mirror across the foyer. She truly looked like a princess. The tiara sparkled in her hair. The champagne-colored gown moved against her like a whisper. This time, even her shoes were perfect, the twenty-first-century version of glass slippers. Beautiful, rather uncomfortable and very, very expensive.

But she would have done anything to go back in time to when she was just a plain, poor secretary, happy in Maksim's arms and bed. Back to when they'd actually had a chance at happiness.

Back to when he'd loved her. He'd never said the words then, but he'd made her feel them.

Grace saw Maksim's sister waiting for them at the bottom of the stairs. Dariya glowed as she hugged them both. "I'm so glad you're my sister," she whispered to Grace. "Not just my sister...my friend. And you're going to make me an aunt!"

"Thank you." Blinking back tears, Grace did her best to smile. "Your friendship means so much..."

She froze when she saw Lady Francesca Danvers over Dariya's shoulder.

She felt her husband stiffen beside her. She glanced at him. His face had closed down, his mouth a grim line, as he looked straight at Francesca.

"Excuse me," he said shortly.

Grace watched as he crossed through the crowd, grabbed the redhead's wrist and dragged her toward his study. His expression looked furious as he closed the door behind him.

And staring at the closed door, everything suddenly became clear for Grace.

He wasn't having an affair with Francesca. She now knew that to her core. He'd promised fidelity to Grace and he would keep to that vow. He was a man of honor.

He hadn't invited her here. He was determined to remain faithful to the wife he'd never wanted. Family and honor meant everything to Maksim. He would remain faithful to Grace.

But did she want him to?

After so many years of being Alan's doormat, desperate for any sign of tenderness, did she really want to be tied forever to a man who didn't love her?

And worse: did she want to raise their child that way?

Could she raise her baby to be happy in this palace of ice? Could she risk her child's bright, joyful new spirit in this frozen place, knowing he'd always be bewildered by his parents' cold misery and might eventually blame himself?

Grace may have sacrificed herself for her baby's sake, but she couldn't allow the life and warmth to be sapped out of her newborn's soul. She couldn't allow her precious baby to grow up suffocated in an endless winter of unspoken blame.

"What's *she* doing here?" Dariya said sourly. "Can't the woman take a hint?"

"I...I'm not feeling very well," Grace said, rubbing her forehead. "Will you please make my excuses and thank everyone for coming?"

"Of course, absolutely." Dariya peered at her in worry. "You do look pale. I'll go get my brother—"

"No! Don't tell him anything. I want to be alone." She ran upstairs with a hard lump in her throat.

Slamming her bedroom door behind her, she collapsed on her bed.

Love made a family.

She loved their baby. She loved Maksim.

But Maksim loved Francesca.

Grace's eyes fell on her battered old suitcase in the massive walk-in closet. It had taken her to London, back to California, to Moscow. It could take her back home.

"If you love him, let him go," Francesca had said.

Grace loved Maksim. She loved her baby. She loved them both so much and there was only one way to save them. One way to make sure they were both safe and happy. One way to set them both free.

Rising from the bed, she picked up her suitcase.

"How dare you show up here?" Maksim said furiously as he closed the study door behind them. "I expressly told you in London—we're through. We were done two and a half months ago when you gave me your little ultimatum."

Francesca looked up at him with her perfectly lined

green eyes. "But I made up for that, darling, when I got the merger back for you!"

"You only gave back something that should always have been mine."

A tremulous smile traced her red mouth. "I rectified a strategic misfire. You won this round."

He stared at her coldly. He expected at any moment, tears would appear—her carefully manufactured tears that never smudged her eye makeup. She was a master at manipulation.

Unlike Grace. Grace who'd looked so vulnerable just moments before they came down the stairway. She'd truly looked like a princess.

"I love you," she'd said. "Can you ever love me?"

His reply to her had been harsh.

Maksim clenched his hands, remembering the stricken look on her face. Grace had no defenses. It had been coldhearted and cruel of him. But she'd kept pushing him for what he wouldn't, couldn't give her...

"Come back with me to London," Francesca said. "It's time."

"Perhaps you haven't noticed," he replied acidly, "but I have a wife."

Emotion turned her thin face pale beneath the rouge. "I never should have given you an ultimatum. But how long do you intend to punish me for my mistake? Let the gold digger go."

"What did you call her?" he said dangerously.

She threw him a scornful glance. "Oh, please. A secretary? She's obviously a gold digger. I just offered her a blank check to leave you, but she refused. She knows she can cash in for more after the little brat is born!"

He clenched his fists. "You tried to buy her off?"

She sniffed. "I was trying to do you a favor, darling. You can't actually want to be married to her. She's not remotely your type!"

His type?

Pictures of Grace went through his mind. Her openness. Her purity. Her laughter and her tears. The way her thoughts were always revealed on her face. Her care and concern for the people around her. Her soft heart.

Gold digger? She'd made it clear from the beginning that she didn't want Maksim's money. He'd tried to spoil her in London, but she'd made it impossible. Over and over again, she'd refused his offers of gifts for clothes, jewels, cars, houses.

The only time she'd accepted anything was to give her family a place to live, when Maksim had black-mailed her into marriage. A strange feeling almost like shame went through him at the memory.

I had no choice, he told himself. *I had to protect my child. I had to make her marry me.* But the oft-repeated reason rang hollow today.

"I love you," she'd whispered. "Can you ever love me?"

"You're right," he said heavily, clawing his hand through his dark hair. "Grace is not my usual type of woman."

"She's not." Francesca gave him a sly smile. "I am."

She was right. Francesca was exactly his type. A selfish beauty who enjoyed playing games and liked to fight dirty. She liked to insinuate they were special due to aristocratic birth, but there was one thing and one thing only Francesca thought was truly noble: money.

Creeping closer to him, she licked her sultry red lips. "You and I are perfect for each other. Yes, we fought constantly, but only because we pursue our own desires no matter the cost. We're both selfish to the bone. Face it, Maksim, we're exactly alike!"

He stared at her.

"That's not true," he said hoarsely. "I'm nothing like you. Now get out."

"Maksim, don't be a fool. You're throwing away a fortune if you don't marry me!"

"We're done, Francesca. Through." He clenched his fists, staring at her coldly. "If I ever see you again—if you ever upset my wife again—you will regret it." Walking to the door, he flung it open. "Now leave."

"Fine," she ground out, tossing her head and exiting toward the curious party-goers outside. "Enjoy your common little wife. You'll be tired of her before your kid's even born!"

In the echo of her departing steps, Maksim closed the door heavily and sank into a chair at his desk. In his heart of hearts, he knew that he *was* just like Francesca.

Or at least he had been. Until he'd met someone who'd inspired him. Someone who with her sweet kindness and natural beauty had made him believe there was more to life than money.

He heard someone come in, and looked up, ready to snarl.

His sister stood in the doorway, her arms folded.

"About time you sent that woman away," Dariya said.

"And I hope you did it more thoroughly this time. Heaven knows she won't take a hint. Maybe you should toss a Rolex into the Moskva River—she'd be sure to dive through the ice. That would be one way to finally—"

"Where's Grace?" he interrupted.

"She wasn't feeling well, so she's gone upstairs to her room." Her eyes met his. "You have a houseful of guests with no host or hostess at the moment. I thought you'd want to know."

He took a deep breath. "Did Grace see me come in here with Francesca?"

"Yes. Everyone saw it. You might want to come and do some damage control."

Maksim clenched his jaw. "I'll go to her now." His encounter with Francesca had left him feeling strangely dirty. Had he really been like that? *Like her?*

He needed to see Grace. To see her calm face and hear her sweet voice. To have her take him in her soft arms so that he could take a deep, clear breath...

"Let Grace rest, Maksim," Dariya said sharply. "Let her sleep and talk to her in the morning. You need to end the rumors going through Moscow, or your marriage will be over before it's begun."

He clenched his jaw. He didn't blame Grace for fleeing to her bedroom. How could he? He'd left her alone during their wedding reception, abandoning her with hundreds of strangers while he disappeared behind closed doors with his ex-mistress.

No wonder Grace had been so insecure, considering that he hadn't bothered to reassure her. He'd just left her, his lonely, pregnant, deserted wife.

He clenched his hands into fists.

He had to make this right.

He had to see her.

"We're exactly alike," Francesca had said.

But fighting that was the soft echo of Grace's voice from long ago. "You're a good man, Maksim. You think it's weakness…but I know your secret."

Which woman did he want to believe?

Which man did he want to be?

He took a deep breath. "I'll just check on her. I won't wake her if she's sleeping," he promised. "Act as hostess until I'm back, Daritchka, won't you?"

But friends and acquaintances were swarming the foyer. Bewildered at the sudden abrupt disappearance of both bride and groom, they stopped him in his path, asking for reassurance and explanations that Maksim hardly knew how to give. It took him almost twenty minutes to cross the marble floor of the foyer to the limestone stairs.

He went to Grace's bedroom and knocked softly on the door. When he heard no answer, he pushed the door open.

Her room was dark. Only in the faintest trace of moonlight from the window could he see her shape in the Wedgwood-blue canopy bed beneath the covers.

He wanted to wake her but held himself back. Waking her would be selfish when it was only to seek his own comfort.

He was a husband.

He was going to be a father.

Everything had changed for him, but he'd been slow to realize it.

Turning away, ignoring the ache in his throat, he went downstairs and did his duty as host. He spent the rest of the long night entertaining his guests and reassuring them that his new bride had just taken ill due to her delicate condition. But all through the endless hours, he couldn't stop thinking of his pregnant wife sleeping upstairs. Lonely in the bedroom that he'd given her as a way to punish her for calling his offer of marriage "a gilded cage."

At dawn, after he'd finally shoved the last guest firmly out the door, Maksim crept back to her room, praying she would now be awake. If she wasn't awake, he didn't know how much longer he could wait.

He needed to feel comforted by her presence. To tell her he was sorry he'd been so cruel. To tell her…to tell her…

The warm blush of a gray-and-pink dawn filled her bedroom as he pushed open the door. She was still in bed, just as she'd been before.

I won't wake her, he told himself. He would just watch her sleep. Even that would bring him some small peace.

But as he walked forward in the lightening room, something didn't look right. Her body beneath the blanket looked strange. The comforter stretched all the way up to the headboard. He pulled back the blanket and discovered…pillows.

She was gone!

He snatched up the note attached to the pillow. It read:

Maksim,
There is no baby. I faked the pregnancy—don't

ask how—to try and get your money. But I can't do it. Please divorce me immediately and don't try to find me. I don't want any alimony. I wish you every happiness in your life with Francesca. All I want is for you to be with the woman you love.

Grace

No baby? She'd faked the pregnancy?

Pain ripped through him, pain so staggering it almost dropped him to his knees.

He couldn't breathe. The tie on his tuxedo suddenly seemed to constrict his air, choking him. He ripped it to the ground in a tear of fabric. He read the note again. And again.

No baby.

She'd faked the pregnancy.

He crumpled up the note in his fist.

He'd been shocked by her pregnancy, but until this moment he hadn't realized how much the baby had come to mean to him. In spare moments between the bone-crushing work of completing the oil company merger, he'd daydreamed about their coming baby. Would he have the Rostov profile? Would he have Grace's pale-blond hair and blue eyes?

He threw the note across the room. It floated gently to the floor. Not enough. Grabbing the lamp, he threw it across the room, smashing it against the wall.

No baby.

She'd lied to him. She'd faked the pregnancy to marry him for his...

Money?

His body snapped straight. Grace, after his money?

He recalled all the times he'd tried to help Grace with money. She'd refused. She'd fought everything—jewels, designer clothes, fancy cars, cash, everything. Beyond having food, clothes and a roof over their heads, Grace didn't give a damn about the so-called finer things in life. All the designer clothes and jewels she'd gotten since their marriage were still hanging neatly in her closet. His eyes fell upon the priceless tiara once owned by his great-aunt, the Grand Duchess.

Grace hadn't lied about the baby.

She was lying now.

He looked back at the note.

Please divorce me immediately and don't try to find me. I don't want any alimony. All I want is for you to be with the woman you love.

Francesca must have somehow convinced Grace that Maksim loved her.

And he'd helped her, he acknowledged to himself grimly. He thought of all the times he could have reassured Grace that he wanted both her and the child. The hours he could have spent with Grace, instead of deserting her in his palace. He'd claimed he wanted to protect his unborn son or daughter, and he'd forced Grace to be his wife, but he'd never acted like a decent husband or father.

He'd withheld the security and comfort and affection he could have given his lonely, pregnant wife.

Grace, on the other hand, wanted him to be happy—

even if that meant throwing him into the arms of another woman.

Shame raced through him, and this time he couldn't deny the emotion for what it was.

He didn't deserve Grace's love. He didn't deserve her.

But...he *loved* her.

She was like no other woman he'd ever known. Her faith and honesty. Her willingness to sacrifice herself for others. *He loved her.* He loved her and he'd let his anger and hurt pride get in the way of his own happiness...and hers.

How could he have been such a blind, selfish fool?

Maksim had money, power, influence—everything he'd ever wanted when he'd been desperately poor as a child. But all his success had somehow become meaningless without her.

What use was it to be one of the wealthiest men in the world, if he didn't have the woman he loved?

CHAPTER TWELVE

GRACE rubbed the frost off the edges of the train window and looked out at Lake Baikal and the distant mountains. The endless white of the deepest lake in the world was an eerie expanse of snow. Hillocks of razor-sharp ice, ten feet tall, stabbed upward on the edges of the frozen lake.

How many days had she been on the train? Her journey from Moscow blended together in endless dark days and still darker nights. She looked numbly at the tiny village with a few wooden buildings scattered up the hillside. Grace couldn't read the Cyrillic letters on the sign to even know its name.

Siberia.

She'd hoped taking the Trans-Siberian Railway would raise her desolate spirits, as well as make sure that Maksim couldn't find her. He would check at the airport and possibly trains heading west into Europe. He wouldn't look here.

If he bothered to look for her at all.

Her body felt hot in the sweltering train car as she

leaned her forehead against the steamy, half-frosted window. But instead of enjoying her childhood dream, she couldn't stop agonizing about the man she'd left behind.

This train station was just a small platform covered with snow, on which three women wrapped in coats and hats were selling fish, homemade bread and fruit to train passengers. After so many days spent weeping in her packed third-class compartment, hanging out of the window and trying not to smell the stale smoke and sweat, Grace saw oranges and suddenly hungered for the sweet tangy fruit as fiercely and recklessly as Rapunzel's mother had once longed for rampion in the fairy tale.

Putting her thick coat over her old jeans and sweater, she crawled out of her upper berth and got off the train. She traded a few Russian coins to the old woman in furs, then snatched up the fruit. Grace barely managed to peel off half of the rind before she sank her mouth into the juicy fruit. Tears streamed down her face. It was delicious. It was heaven.

But by the next bite, the orange had suddenly lost its flavor. She stared out at the vast white emptiness of the snow-covered lake and craved something far more.

Her husband.

Her heart twisted in her chest every time she thought of how she'd left him. How she'd lied to him!

I was right to lie about the pregnancy, she told herself. *He doesn't really want to be a husband or a father. I can't keep him from the woman he loves. Not when I all I want is his happiness, and our child's...*

But at this moment she wanted Maksim so badly she

could hardly believe she'd had the strength of will to be so unselfish. She yearned for him. For his touch. For his smile. Even for his haughty glare. She would have taken any and all of it.

The night of the reception, she'd snuck out of the house and managed to sell her mother's wedding ring for the equivalent of a hundred dollars in a pawn shop near Yaroslavskiy Station in the center of the city.

Every day of her journey had been full of tears. She couldn't stop thinking about Maksim in love with another woman...thinking of the fact that she'd sold her mother's wedding ring...thinking of her own unborn child who would have no father.

The kindly Russian *provodnika* who was in charge of their train car had grown so concerned she'd started sneaking Grace dried fish and borscht from the first-class dining car. An invisible alliance of women who'd been hurt in love.

Grace wondered suddenly if everyone on earth was secretly hiding a broken heart.

She stared blindly across the white snowy expanse of Lake Baikal. In the distance she saw a black truck driving across the frozen lake toward her. The image blurred as her eyes filled with tears.

She hated what she'd done. How she'd lied to him.

It was the only way to set him free, she tried to tell herself. She wiped her tears with the back of a gloved hand. If Maksim knew their unborn child still lived, flourishing and growing every day inside her, he would have tracked her down to the ends of the earth. And she would not have been able to give him his freedom.

Now her own freedom stretched before her like a death sentence. In a few days, at the end of the tracks, she would reach Vladivostok. From there she'd get cheap passage across the Pacific. She would find some kind of job and raise her child in California's endless sunny days.

And yet the thought of that sunshine was more bleak to her than any rain.

As she took a deep shuddering breath, the black truck whirled to a stop on the other side of the platform in a scatter of snow and ice.

A dark figure come out of it, slamming the door with a hard bang.

He walked toward her, a dark prince coming from the white mist like a Gothic warlord with a long black coat, surrounded by snow and jagged sharp ice like ancient swords left by northern giants.

The orange dropped from her nerveless hands as he reached her.

"Maksim…?" she whispered.

Taking her in his arms, he kissed her fiercely.

"Grace, oh, Grace," he whispered. "Thank God. I was afraid I would never find you."

"But what are you doing here? In Siberia?" Still believing that she was dreaming, she reached up to touch his rough cheek. It was thick with bristle. She'd never seen him so unkempt. "You haven't shaved…"

"This train was my last hope. Oh God. I've barely slept for the last four days. Thank God I've found you." She thought she saw a suspicious glimmer in his eyes as he stroked her cheek. He lifted her chin. "Both of you."

She gasped. He knew she'd been lying!

She tried to open her mouth to lie to his beautiful, powerful face, but she couldn't do it. A sob rose to her lips.

"I'm…sorry," she cried, pressing her face against his chest.

"Sorry?" he said gently, rubbing her back. "Oh, *solnishka mayo*. I am the one who is sorry."

"I tried so hard to let you go," she sobbed. "I wanted you to be happy, and I've failed…."

"Failed?" He laughed softly, shaking his head. "Don't you think I know you by now? You have a heart as big as the world. I knew almost at once that you were trying to sacrifice your own happiness for mine."

"Just as you once sacrificed what you wanted most for my sake." Tears streamed down her face, wet tears that stung as they froze like hoarfrost against her skin. "But, Maksim, I want you to be with the woman you love—"

"I *am* with the woman I love," he said fiercely. He forced her to meet his eyes, and she couldn't look away from the intensity of his gaze, a whirling blend of black and white, of snow and hot steel. "It's you, Grace. Only you. The only woman I have ever loved. The only woman I will ever love."

"Me?" she whispered, hardly daring to believe she'd heard him right.

"My plane is waiting at a private airstrip across the lake." He put his arm over her shoulders. "Let us go home."

"Home." The thought tantalized her. She looked up at him. "Are you sure?"

"I wish to make one thing clear, *solnishka mayo*." Reaching for her hand, he pressed it against his rough cheek. "I didn't marry you just because you were pregnant. Even when I thought I hated you, part of me always knew you were the only one for me. Now I will be yours to the end. You are my princess. My wife." He put his hand on his heart. "I love you with all my heart, and I always will."

And to her incredulous wonder, he kissed her passionately on the train platform on the edge of the misty Siberian forest and endless white lake.

As if from a distance, she heard a burst of applause, then yells in Russian, Chinese and a few other languages she couldn't recognize. Blushing, Grace pulled away from Maksim to see people young and old hanging out of the sliding windows on the train, beaming down at the two lovers, clearly egging them on.

She saw the impish look on Maksim's face as he wrapped them both in his black coat.

"Today is January sixth," he whispered. "Do you know what day that is?"

She licked her lips. "Epiphany?"

"It's also Christmas Eve."

"Christmas Eve was weeks ago!"

"Russians celebrate Christmas on January seventh. One Christmas isn't enough for a winter as long as ours." He glanced back mischievously at the people cheering and hanging out of the train windows. "So let us give our audience one last gift for the season." He stroked her cold cheek, unfreezing her tears with the warmth of his breath. "Let's show them what love really means."

And this time, when he kissed her, it was so long and deep and true that she couldn't hear the applause or the whistle of the train. She couldn't hear anything but the pounding of her own heart roaring in her ears, in perfect rhythm with his.

A year later Grace crept down the holly-decked stairs in their Devonshire house, weighed down with Christmas stockings.

She heard a noise in the room below and froze. She knew her brothers were far too old to believe in Santa, but she had baby Sergey to think about now. Then she giggled at the thought that her four-month-old son might catch her. He was certainly the smartest, cleverest baby on earth, but that was pushing it a little too far, even for a proud mother.

Santa had already brought Grace everything she'd ever wanted.

She only had to look around this house. The country house had seemed so empty and wistful last year when she and Maksim had first conceived Sergey. But not anymore. She'd spent the last few months of her pregnancy consulting designers, buying furniture from all over the world, making it comfortable and bright. She'd done the same for their other homes in Moscow, London, Los Angeles, Cap Ferrat and Antigua, but this house was her favorite.

This house was their home.

She'd gone into labor three weeks early here, while finishing the baby's nursery. Sergey had been born at the hospital in a nearby village at a healthy seven pounds three ounces, and he'd been growing ever since. The baby was happy here and so were his parents. Grace could feel the house glowing with happiness, the wood of the banister warm beneath her touch as she came downstairs to the family room with the old fireplace and their Christmas tree.

She stopped when she saw her husband, still shirt-less as he'd slept and wearing only the bright red reindeer flannel pajama pants she'd bought him as a joke, walking their baby son back and forth in front of the shining lights of their twelve-foot Christmas tree.

"He's finally asleep," Maksim whispered, and kissed their baby son tenderly on top of his downy head. "I'll take him up to bed."

She nodded with a lump in her throat. As she watched her husband carry their slumbering baby up the stair-case, she wondered what she'd ever done to deserve such happiness. All her dreams had come true.

For her Christmas surprise, Maksim had flown her whole family here from California yesterday to share their baby's first Christmas.

"Oh, my dear," her mother had whispered to her last night, her eyes full of joyful tears as they shared their midnight cocoa, "you're really going to live happily ever after."

Now Grace hung the red stockings—stuffed full of candy, oranges and small gifts—on the marble mantel and stood back to see the effect. She nodded with satis-faction, then placed one last gift in her mother's stocking. Her father's wedding ring. Maksim had tracked it down for her in Moscow two weeks ago. Grace had cried with gratitude, kissing him again and again.

She glanced down at her left hand, which now shone

with a ten-carat diamond surrounded by sapphires, set in gold with a matching wedding band. Maksim had given it to her right after she'd kissed him. "To match your hair and eyes." He'd added with a wicked grin, "I know this time it's a gift you can't refuse."

And she hadn't refused. She couldn't. It fit perfectly with the wedding ring that meant everything to her, the one he'd bought her on Russia's Christmas day last year. She was so happy and proud to be his wife.

And she'd finally found the perfect gift to give him in return. The perfect Christmas present for the man who had everything.

Smiling through the tears, Grace gently placed the small gift in Maksim's stocking. It was a small framed picture of baby Sergey she'd taken last night, while Maksim was in the village doing last-minute Christmas shopping. In the photo, the baby was wearing a T-shirt she'd made herself, with words that read, "I'm going to be a big brother."

Looking at the stocking, picturing Maksim's reaction, she smiled, and tears welled up in her eyes. *Such a ninny I am,* she thought, wiping her eyes and laughing at herself. But was it possible to die of happiness?

Upstairs she could hear her younger brothers waking up. In a moment they would be racing downstairs to open their presents beneath the tree. Her mother would bustle around the enormous, refurbished kitchen, insisting on cooking brunch for them as the staff had the day off. Then she'd sit by the fire, knitting booties for the baby while studying books for next semester's classes.

And Grace could sit on her husband's lap and kiss

him when no one was looking. He would kiss her back, and they would wait with breathless anticipation for their private Christmas celebrations to come during the silent, sacred night.

With a grateful breath, Grace glanced outside through the tall windows at the wide expanse of white fields, the peaceful moment before the world woke. Outside, the first rays of pink dawn were streaking through black trees covered with snow.

It was the winter glow of her heart. Even in the stillness of winter they would forever have the warmth and light of home. And as she heard her husband's step on the stairs coming back to her, she knew the sunshine would always last.

MILLS & BOON

AUGUST 2009 HARDBACK TITLES

ROMANCE

Desert Prince, Bride of Innocence	Lynne Graham
Raffaele: Taming His Tempestuous Virgin	Sandra Marton
The Italian Billionaire's Secretary Mistress	Sharon Kendrick
Bride, Bought and Paid For	Helen Bianchin
Hired for the Boss's Bedroom	Cathy Williams
The Christmas Love-Child	Jennie Lucas
Mistress to the Merciless Millionaire	Abby Green
Italian Boss, Proud Miss Prim	Susan Stephens
Proud Revenge, Passionate Wedlock	Janette Kenny
The Buenos Aires Marriage Deal	Maggie Cox
Betrothed: To the People's Prince	Marion Lennox
The Bridesmaid's Baby	Barbara Hannay
The Greek's Long-Lost Son	Rebecca Winters
His Housekeeper Bride	Melissa James
A Princess for Christmas	Shirley Jump
The Frenchman's Plain-Jane Project	Myrna Mackenzie
Italian Doctor, Dream Proposal	Margaret McDonagh
Marriage Reunited: Baby on the Way	Sharon Archer

HISTORICAL

The Brigadier's Daughter	Catherine March
The Wicked Baron	Sarah Mallory
His Runaway Maiden	June Francis

MEDICAL™

Wanted: A Father for her Twins	Emily Forbes
Bride on the Children's Ward	Lucy Clark
The Rebel of Penhally Bay	Caroline Anderson
Marrying the Playboy Doctor	Laura Iding

MILLS & BOON

AUGUST 2009 LARGE PRINT TITLES

ROMANCE

The Spanish Billionaire's Pregnant Wife	Lynne Graham
The Italian's Ruthless Marriage Command	Helen Bianchin
The Brunelli Baby Bargain	Kim Lawrence
The French Tycoon's Pregnant Mistress	Abby Green
Diamond in the Rough	Diana Palmer
Secret Baby, Surprise Parents	Liz Fielding
The Rebel King	Melissa James
Nine-to-Five Bride	Jennie Adams

HISTORICAL

The Disgraceful Mr Ravenhurst	Louise Allen
The Duke's Cinderella Bride	Carole Mortimer
Impoverished Miss, Convenient Wife	Michelle Styles

MEDICAL™

Children's Doctor, Society Bride	Joanna Neil
The Heart Surgeon's Baby Surprise	Meredith Webber
A Wife for the Baby Doctor	Josie Metcalfe
The Royal Doctor's Bride	Jessica Matthews
Outback Doctor, English Bride	Leah Martyn
Surgeon Boss, Surprise Dad	Janice Lynn

MILLS & BOON®

SEPTEMBER 2009 HARDBACK TITLES

ROMANCE

A Bride for His Majesty's Pleasure	Penny Jordan
The Master Player	Emma Darcy
The Infamous Italian's Secret Baby	Carole Mortimer
The Millionaire's Christmas Wife	Helen Brooks
Duty, Desire and the Desert King	Jane Porter
Royal Love-Child, Forbidden Marriage	Kate Hewitt
One-Night Mistress...Convenient Wife	Anne McAllister
Prince of Montéz, Pregnant Mistress	Sabrina Philips
The Count of Castelfino	Christina Hollis
Beauty and the Billionaire	Barbara Dunlop
Crowned: The Palace Nanny	Marion Lennox
Christmas Angel for the Billionaire	Liz Fielding
Under the Boss's Mistletoe	Jessica Hart
Jingle-Bell Baby	Linda Goodnight
The Magic of a Family Christmas	Susan Meier
Mistletoe & Marriage	Patricia Thayer & Donna Alward
Her Baby Out of the Blue	Alison Roberts
A Doctor, A Nurse: A Christmas Baby	Amy Andrews

HISTORICAL

Devilish Lord, Mysterious Miss	Annie Burrows
To Kiss a Count	Amanda McCabe
The Earl and the Governess	Sarah Elliott

MEDICAL™

Country Midwife, Christmas Bride	Abigail Gordon
Greek Doctor: One Magical Christmas	Meredith Webber
Spanish Doctor, Pregnant Midwife	Anne Fraser
Expecting a Christmas Miracle	Laura Iding

 **MILLS & BOON**

SEPTEMBER 2009 LARGE PRINT TITLES

ROMANCE

The Sicilian Boss's Mistress — Penny Jordan
Pregnant with the Billionaire's Baby — Carole Mortimer
The Venadicci Marriage Vengeance — Melanie Milburne
The Ruthless Billionaire's Virgin — Susan Stephens
Italian Tycoon, Secret Son — Lucy Gordon
Adopted: Family in a Million — Barbara McMahon
The Billionaire's Baby — Nicola Marsh
Blind-Date Baby — Fiona Harper

HISTORICAL

Lord Braybrook's Penniless Bride — Elizabeth Rolls
A Country Miss in Hanover Square — Anne Herries
Chosen for the Marriage Bed — Anne O'Brien

MEDICAL™

The Children's Doctor's Special Proposal — Kate Hardy
English Doctor, Italian Bride — Carol Marinelli
The Doctor's Baby Bombshell — Jennifer Taylor
Emergency: Single Dad, Mother Needed — Laura Iding
The Doctor Claims His Bride — Fiona Lowe
Assignment: Baby — Lynne Marshall